PENGU

MAMI SUZUK

Simon Rowe left the green hills of New Zealand for the big sky country of Australia when he was sixteen years old. At twenty-one, he set out for the world and somehow managed to fund his travels by photographing and writing about them. He has lived in Japan for more than twenty-five years, winning numerous awards for his short fiction and screenplays, including *Good Night Papa* (2013 Asian Short Screenplay Contest) and *Pearl City: Stories from Japan and Elsewhere* (2021 Best Indie Book Award). His stories about Japanese life and culture have appeared in The Paris Review, the New York Times, TIME (Asia), the South China Morning Post, The Straits Times, The Australian, and the Australian Financial Review. He has a black belt in *iaido* (sword quick-drawing), a passion for sea kayaking, and an itch for adventure he never seems able to scratch.

Mami Suzuki:

Private Eye

Simon Rowe

PENGUIN BOOKS
An imprint of Penguin Random House

PENGUIN BOOKS

USA | Canada | UK | Ireland | Australia
New Zealand | India | South Africa | China | Southeast Asia

Penguin Books is part of the Penguin Random House group of companies
whose addresses can be found at global.penguinrandomhouse.com

Published by Penguin Random House SEA Pte Ltd
9, Changi South Street 3, Level 08-01,
Singapore 486361

First published in Penguin Books by Penguin Random House SEA 2023

ISBN 9789815058895

Typeset in Garamond by MAP Systems, Bengaluru, India

www.penguin.sg

For Masami

Contents

JAPAN

SEA OF JAPAN

Matsue • • Mihonoseki
Himeji • ■ Kobe
Manabeshima • ● Osaka

★ Tokyo

PACIFIC OCEAN

Ishigakijima •

N

Pearl City

Silhouetted against the noon sky, the president of Tokai Pearls Limited stood at his suite window and surveyed the harbour. His gaze shifted from the shipyards and submarine docks of Kawasaki Heavy Industries to the Mosaic Shopping Mall and its slow-turning Ferris wheel, then to Port Tower where tour boats came and went from the ferry terminal, and finally to the Rokko mountains that lifted the suburbs in a great pale wave above the Seto Inland Sea.

'Do you know why they call this Pearl City?' he said.

The three dark suits at the back of the room said nothing. Their collective gaze instead fell on the middle-aged woman in a blue pantsuit who sat on the leather sofa chair in front of them. She was generously built, wore her jet-black hair in a bob, and rested her manicured hands on the chestnut brown handbag on her lap.

'Because pearls are a Kobe girl's best friend?' she ventured.

The president boomed. His laughter rolled about the room like distant thunder. 'Good, good! I like it,' he said, then to the back of the room, 'Mr Danno, make a note of that. We could use it in advertising.'

A slim young man with a fashionable hairstyle gave a curt 'Hai!', drew a pen from his breast pocket and scribbled into a notepad.

1

The president seated himself behind a desk of polished walnut—a pink conch shell paperweight to one side and a speed-dial phone to the other. He was a short man, heavy-set, with a cherubic face and a smooth, tanned pate that caught the sunlight at such an angle it made him look almost angelic.

'I'll tell you why it's called Pearl City, Ms Suzuki,' he responded. 'Because more pearls pass through this town than anywhere else in the world, and more pearls pass through this company than any other in this town. Our reputation, like our pearls, is unblemished.' He leaned forward. 'That is why we have asked you here today.'

Suzuki glanced about the room. She noted the reproductions of old photos showing pearl luggers, turn-of-the-century fishing villages, and half-naked female divers—the famed 'sea women' of Mie Prefecture. She noted the brass diving bell helmet set on the teakwood sideboard, the mounted stag horn of red coral, and the framed photo of the Empress of Japan around whose neck gleamed three strands of fine Akoya pearls. Her gaze returned to the president.

'Someone is stealing from me, and I want to know who,' he said, then nodded towards the young man behind her. 'Mr Danno here is my assistant….'

'Thank you for coming, Ms Suzuki,' Danno said, stepping lightly across the room to his boss's side. 'You come highly recommended.'

'Oh?' she said.

'You did some work for my wife's sister a few months ago … a Ms Deguchi?'

Suzuki's eyebrows arched. 'The underwear thief case?'

'She said you're a fast worker. "Very intuitive" were the words she used.'

'I had some help—'

'Nevertheless,' the president interrupted, 'there are one hundred and twelve staff in this company, nearly all of them female. We believe a female detective, such as yourself, stands a better chance of finding the thief than the Kobe Metropolitan Police. We are offering you three-hundred-thousand yen, paid upfront. An additional three-hundred thousand will be for proof of the thief's identity.' He nodded at Danno, who reached into his breast pocket and produced a brown envelope that he passed on to her.

She felt the tight wad of crisp banknotes inside and drew a breath—more than a month's salary in her hands. She looked up and her gaze was arrested by the image of a solo free diver on the wall behind the president. She was full-breasted and strong-armed, wearing only a loincloth as she descended the depths on shafts of sunlight. Suzuki had heard that the 'sea women' of Mie could stay down longer than men—their extra body fat kept them from freezing. She wondered how much a woman like that had been paid for her time and effort.

'Ms Suzuki?' said Danno. 'May we have your answer, please?'

Her gaze returned to the two men and she breathed out slowly.

* * *

The Tokai Pearls Limited building stood at the end of the esplanade, a handsome six-storey monolith of sandstone and steel that had miraculously survived the American air raids of the Pacific War. The pearl-sorting rooms were located on the second- and third-floors. Their wide windows ran along the length of the harbour-facing side which—as Danno explained—allowed the pearl graders to take full advantage of the natural light.

They stopped halfway along a corridor, and Suzuki peered through the porthole window of a door labelled 'B Section'. Dozens of women in powder blue uniforms and matching hats bearing the Tokai Pearls insignia hunched over their workstations, dexterously scooping pearls from small blue buckets and placing them on sorting mats. They held each pearl to the light with a set of digital callipers, rotated it slowly for a few moments, then placed it into one of several containers.

'Pearls are assessed for their size, colour, lustre, shape, and surface,' said Danno.

'Are they paid well?'

'The graders? Two hundred and eighty thousand yen is their starting salary.'

'May I see one of the workstations?'

He glanced at his watch. 'D Section is on a tea break. Follow me.'

They took the stairwell to the third-floor and stopped at a door identical to the first. Danno swiped his access card and they stepped inside. Clear, bright light bathed the room and the air smelled faintly of chemicals. It reminded Suzuki of a veterinarian clinic or a school science lab.

She seated herself at a workstation near a window and examined the table where all paraphernalia—the sorting tray, the calliper, tweezer, loupe stand as well as the rubber gloves and alcohol spray dispensers—were arranged neatly on the white table before her. She glanced up at the CCTV cameras on the ceiling, then down at the blue plastic bucket filled with pearls beside her. The set-up reminded her of a pachinko parlour, the kind that one passed in downtown alleys, where patrons sat dumbly for hours, amassing buckets of ball bearings that they exchanged for cash at a mouse-hole window outside.

'May I?' she asked.

'Be my guest,' Danno said.

She plunged her hand into the bucket, gathered a handful and held them to the light. Then she let them slip between her fingers, feeling their coolness and listening to the music they made as they tumbled back into the bucket.

'Where do they go from here?' she asked.

'To the pearl masters on the fifth-floor. Six qualified gemologists make the final selections.'

'And then?'

'Then the highest quality pearls are barcoded and given ID numbers. After that, they're threaded into strands for sale.'

'How do you know if any are missing?'

'Until they reach the pearl masters, we don't.'

'You don't?'

'Thousands of pearls move through here each week, too many to be counted individually....'

'And those that don't make the cut?'

'Sold at auctions. Mostly to local Chinese and Indian gem traders.'

Suzuki gazed out the window. Sighting the wave-like profile of the Orient Hotel on the far side of the harbour, she glanced at her watch and gasped. 'Final question,' she said, gathering her bag and rising quickly from the workstation. 'Have any pearls *ever* been stolen?'

'The president is a very suspicious man....'

'Has he ever been proven right?'

Irritation flashed over Danno's face, but in a practised and professional tone, he replied, 'In an uncertain world, Ms Suzuki, there are people who will pay for certainty.'

* * *

Suzuki took a taxi to the Orient Hotel. The previous week's CCTV tapes of the sorting rooms and a memory stick containing personnel files of all the graders, including the gemologists, jiggled in her purse. It was a logical place to start—even if the assignment itself seemed illogical. For there to be a thief, there *must* be a theft. When forty-three pairs of women's underwear disappeared from a neighbourhood's clothes lines, one could be sure it wasn't the sea breeze that had carried them off.

The hotel lobby clock chimed 1 p.m. as Suzuki slipped behind the reception desk and checked the guest register. Despite her growling stomach—the meeting at Tokai Pearls had consumed her entire lunch-hour—she set to work with vigour. A cruise ship had docked at port, disgorging several hundred tourists from Shanghai, and the afternoon passed quickly as she and her colleagues processed the guests and got them settled.

With her shift complete, she left the hotel and hurried along the esplanade. Passing beneath the hourglass-shaped Port Tower, where hobby fishermen cast for rockling and horse mackerel, a voice called out, 'Ms Suzuki!'

She turned to glimpse a man in his mid-fifties. He stood by himself with a fishing rod in one hand, waving at her. Unlike the other old salts, he hadn't gone to seed; he was clean-shaven with cropped silver hair and a strong, tanned face. She flashed him a smile and hurried on.

She took the subway train to Nagata Station, collected her bicycle and made her way up the gentle slopes, through the narrow streets of tightly-packed neighbourhoods and to Octopus Garden kindergarten. There, she roused her four-year-old daughter, Aya, who had been dozing peacefully under the watchful eye of the duty teacher, paid the monthly school fee for lunches and overtime care, and departed.

It was a skilful act, carrying a sleepy child home by bicycle, and she had to ride the brake for most of the way. When the two of them reached the small apartment building standing on a knoll overlooking the urban sprawl, the child's grandmother was waiting on the street.

'Okaerinasai,' she greeted, lifting the youngster from the bicycle. Then to Suzuki, 'How did it go?'

'Cruise ship chaos again,' she said. 'What's for dinner?'

The third-floor apartment smelled of steamed rice, seafood tempura, and roasted green tea. Suzuki changed into tracksuit pants, took a low-malt beer from the fridge, and collapsed into an old massage chair in front of the TV. She awoke to her mother's hand gently rousing her for dinner which she hungrily devoured. Her daughter had already been fed and was asleep in bed. After doing the dishes, she set up her ageing laptop on the kitchen table and inserted the USB containing the Tokai Pearls staff files.

The profile photos were mostly of young women with fresh faces and serious expressions. They hailed from rural villages with names like Taka, Tamba, Ono, Shiso, and Sasayama. They had traded rural oppression for urban crush, drawn to the bright lights and excitement that no backwater boondocks could ever offer a young woman in her prime. Suzuki doubted any one of these youngsters would risk it all to pocket a pearl or two.

By 11 p.m., the apartment was quiet and still. Her mother had long since bathed and gone to bed. Suzuki took another beer from the fridge and turned to the Internet, her notepad beside her. She trawled sites on pearl grading, gem trading, pearl markets, auction sites, and dollar-yen exchange rates. She scribbled like a madwoman, stopping only to take a swig from her beer can and ponder the ever-diminishing likelihood that the president of Tokai Pearls Limited was being ripped off by one of his employees.

And yet, the size and lucrativeness of the pearl trade surprised her. No less than a dozen companies kept offices downtown, and many of these represented industry heavyweights like Tiffany & Co., Cartier, Harry Winston, and Chow Tai Fook.

She drained her beer, thought about getting a third but stopped herself; thirds led to fourths. She took a few moments to view the CCTV footage on her MediaPlayer. The images, although fuzzy, showed nothing more than rows of women in identical uniforms, performing a very mundane task. It made her wonder about the motive of the investigation: was it one man's folly or a savvy businessman's intuition?

* * *

The *Haru-ichiban* blew off the harbour the following night. It brought with it the tang of the sea and salty gusts that set the red lanterns of Chinatown bobbing like fat jellyfish.

Suzuki turned off Nankin-machi Street and into a narrow laneway. The uneven flagstones made this no place for a woman in high heels, but she had been here many times and deftly navigated to the end of the alley where a neon sign announced the Bar Bon Voyage. She paused beneath its orange glow, adjusted her midnight blue one-piece—just a pinch too tight—and pushed on the door. The warm, smoky fog of a Tuesday night washed over her. A chorus of greetings from the staff followed her as she made her way along a long, dark wooden counter. At the very end sat a man with a sake flask and a small cup in front of him. At her approach, he looked up and there it was again—that smile.

'How come you never wave back?' he asked, pulling out her chair.

To the staff she said, 'A beer please,' and in the same breath, 'You know it's nothing personal, Teizo.'

'So it's professional,' he said, returning to his sake cup and pouring himself a fresh drink. 'How's the sleuthing business?'

'How's the fishing business?'

'Like you, I'm only catching small ones.'

Her beer arrived. 'Kampai,' she said, touching the lip of her vessel to his.

'A new case?' he asked.

'Can't talk about it—yet.'

'Can I help?'

'Maybe not.'

'I helped on the panty thief case.'

'You did.' She took a long draught of beer and wiped her lip.

'And I helped you catch the shoplifting granddad.'

'You did.'

'Well, what have you got for me this time?'

'This time I need to get inside a woman's head, not a man's.'

'You came here tonight....'

She let a smile work its way to her lips and sighed. 'This time I might just be chasing fresh air on the wild hunch of a paranoid company president who thinks he's being stolen from.'

'A man?'

'Yes.'

'I'm a man.'

'I've noticed.'

'Remember, a man fears things like a woman. Things that sometimes can't be explained—or proven. Some feel it; some don't.' He took a sip of sake, then another. 'Paranoia is just another word for fear.'

She raised the beer glass to her lips and in the bar mirror caught a glimpse of a middle-aged woman, full-faced, with gleaming black hair. Her eyes were quick, her red lips glistening.

'Do I look like a private eye?'

Most men would have taken advantage of the question to let their gaze linger over her generous proportions, but Teizo looked her in the eye and said, 'No.'

'Good. Then tell me, what's all this *male-fear* business? Did they teach you that at submarine school?'

'Didn't need to. When you're at sea for weeks, months even, you just learn it. You learn to smell fear above and below the surface….'

'You smelt an underwear thief.'

'What I'm saying is, no man is born with instinct. He acquires it. And the faster he acquires it, the better are his chances of survival. Maybe your company president is such a man. Maybe he fears a thief will make him look bad and just needs you to prove there isn't one.' He drained his cup and ordered another drink.

'What do you know about pearls?' she asked.

'Submariners call them mermaid tears.'

'Interesting, but not useful.'

'Then fill me in.'

'Alright then.' She swivelled her chair to face him. 'Why would a young woman, a high school graduate from a rural town, risk a good salary and her name, to steal from the biggest pearl dealer in Asia?'

'Tokai Pearls?'

'Yes.'

The staff returned with fresh sake. He waited for her to leave, then said, 'Pearls aren't just pretty baubles, you know. They have practical uses. Medicine for one. The Chinese use pearl powder to treat skin problems. Chinese royalty used them in beauty creams. In India, they're used to treat stomach aches. There's also pearl tea, a health tonic….'

Meanwhile, Suzuki had taken a pen from her handbag and was scribbling hastily on a bar napkin.

'… never really cared for pearls myself,' he said finally. 'They remind me of weddings and funerals.'

She put down her pen, raised her glass and said, 'I'll drink to that.'

* * *

To save the taxi fare, Suzuki decided to walk. Nankin-machi Street's late-night ramen joints and upstairs karaoke boxes resounded with drunken laughter, but the alleys that branched off it were sullen and cavernous with shadow.

She reached Sakaemachi Road, busy with westbound traffic, and feeling pensive, crossed over and continued south into the old financial precinct. Here, the paved stones were wider, smoother, and the streets carried a whiff of the wealth and history they had accumulated for over a century of international trade. Sandstone and granite towered over her, corniced and classically hewn. Where no insurance company, bank, or shipping office stood, an Armani, Porsche, or Tiffany & Co. showroom glowed like a jewel in rock.

She pondered on Teizo's words—not so much the 'male fear' part but the possibilities that pearls presented. She passed by Mikimoto, the boutique of the famed pearl merchant of Mie; then, stopped and retraced her steps. Peering in at the strands of gleaming Akoya pearls, earrings, brooches, and rings, she couldn't help but repeat to herself Teizo's words, 'pretty baubles'. Ornaments like these were not the fashion statements of young women. They were certainly not the status symbols a pearl company employee would flash around, no less pitch on the open market. She caught herself, aware once more of the possibility that there might not even be a thief, that this could all be a sadistic scheme cooked up by a company president to project power and control over his staff—over her. On the other hand, who was she to complain? The advance would cover kindergarten lunches for six months. And if she *did* catch a thief, well, there was an extra three hundred thousand yen she could put towards her daughter's future.

She continued walking and her thoughts turned again to Teizo. Was theirs a professional relationship—or was it just two lonely hearts sharing a drink in Chinatown on Tuesday nights? She'd paid their bar bill and asked for a receipt; information was a commodity and she valued his learned opinion. But the jury was pending on the true motive of their night-time rendezvous.

After a short while she looked up, startled to see the red hourglass outline of Port Tower looming large against the night sky.

'Damn it,' she hissed.

Resigning herself to the extra cost to save her legs, she hailed a taxi at the next convenience store and slumped back in the seat, watching through heavy eyelids as the peckish, the lonely and the drunk did their best to keep the night alive.

* * *

She awoke around 2 a.m. with her daughter asleep beside her and her mother in the next-door room, emitting a snore that vibrated softly throughout the apartment.

She rose and went to the bathroom, but once back in bed, she could only lie on her back and stare up at the faint but irritating glow of the ceiling 'bean' light. The more she stared at it, the more her mind churned.

That was it!

She leapt from bed and rushed to the kitchen. She turned on the hot water pot and opened her laptop, drumming her fingers on the table until the Tokai Pearls staff files slowly materialized before her. She scrolled downwards, searching the faces of the young women as steam billowed behind her. And there it was: a photo of a woman older than the others, with a gaze more measured and calmer than her fresh-faced colleagues. She had dyed-brown hair, wrapped in a tight, fashionable bun that said she took pride in her appearance. But Suzuki didn't dwell on those details; it was the redness that covered the woman's cheeks, a hot and irritated skin—acne perhaps—which held her attention. She scribbled on her pad as the hot water pot screamed behind and the jar of Nescafé lay untouched.

* * *

'Reiko Ogino?' Danno said, reading the name slowly. 'She's a supervisor in D Section. She's been with us several years now…'

'May I see her at work?' Suzuki said, then quickly, 'She's by no means a suspect….'

Danno smiled wryly. 'We're all suspects, Ms Suzuki. Just some more than others.'

They made their way to the third-floor, stopping outside the grading room Suzuki had inspected two days ago.

'Reiko Ogino is the one standing in the corner,' said Danno.

Suzuki peered through the porthole window and saw a woman speaking with one of the graders seated beside a window on the far side of the room. She strained to see Ogino's face; the angle at which she stood gave away little more than the woman's height and build. She was slim and strong-looking, with an upright posture. The grader said something that made Ogino laugh, pat her subordinate playfully on the arm and turn around. Suzuki uttered a quiet gasp. The face she glimpsed looked quite different to the woman in the file photo.

'Would you like me to call her over? asked Danno.

'No, no,' Suzuki said quickly, turning away. 'I just wanted to see what she looks like. Your staff photos … are they taken only once?'

'Yes. When the employees first enter the company. Why do you ask?'

'What time do they finish?'

'D Section? At 6 p.m.'

Suzuki glanced at her watch. She gave Danno a hurried thank you and left the building. In the taxi, she pulled a rice ball from her handbag and ate quickly, ignoring the curious glances of the driver all the way back to the hotel.

* * *

Teizo was not among the fishers casting from the pier later that day. Even if he had been, she'd not have had time to acknowledge his wave as she hurried along the harbour and back to the company gates of Tokai Pearls Limited. She arrived as the first employees were exiting; young women, laughing and chatting as if the menial tasks they'd just spent hours performing were now a distant memory. Suzuki positioned herself across the road outside a convenience store, a cup of coffee in one hand, a phone in the other, and for effect, pretended to play Tetris.

The workers streamed through the gates. Gone were their formless blue uniforms that had reduced them to a single entity, a human resource to be watered and fed and paid out monthly. They wore fashionable blouses, colourful accessories, boots and form-fitting skirts with bolero denim jackets—clothes that revealed their individuality and character.

Amidst the outflow, Reiko Ogino appeared, sporting a striped blue and white sweatshirt, black jeans and pink Vans sneakers. She broke from the crowd and crossed the street towards the convenience store. Suzuki looked down in panic; she'd forgotten the sleuth's most valued accessory—a face mask! As Ogino reached the store entrance, she made an evasive sidestep to avoid an exiting patron. It brought her close enough for Suzuki to smell her sandalwood fragrance and steal a close glimpse at her face—a face that was radiant, relaxed, and … unblemished.

* * *

The following day, Suzuki attended parents' day at her daughter's kindergarten, taking the morning off work to meet the teachers and chat with the other time-pressed, work-harried parents. They clustered at the back of the classroom listening to their children sing songs about pulling giant radishes, and a story about a boy who marched off to battle demons in a distant land—just like any single mother, Suzuki thought, except that the demons were disguised as beer, bills, and a bad back.

That evening she viewed the CCTV footage again, focusing her attention this time on the happenings inside D Section. Each time Ogino came into view, Suzuki slowed the footage, noting the ease with which the supervisor interacted with her co-workers; in particular, her habit of leaning in close when speaking to the younger employees, her laughing and smiling manner, as if work wasn't the only thing they were discussing.

After an hour, with her eyes strained, Suzuki had to admit there was nothing untoward about the supervisor's behaviour. In fact, Ogino's seemingly compassionate and professional manner impressed her. She went to the fridge and pulled out a beer. Then she remembered: the laundry. With a heavy heart she returned the can, and from the bathroom, lugged a full basket of damp clothes to the balcony. The city shimmered beneath her; a bullet train passed seamlessly through the constellation of streetlights, heading west towards Fukuoka. Out at sea, freighters and night ferries floated like star-ships across the celestial stream, heading east with the tide. It was a view Suzuki could not savour until three generations of women's socks, stockings, and underwear had been strung beneath the moonlight.

* * *

A breakthrough came the next day.

Suzuki, having decided to walk to her dental appointment in Sannomiya, spotted Ogino in Chinatown. Side-stepping into a kitchenware store on Nankin-machi Street, Suzuki pretended to examine the woks and noodle sieves, watching as Ogino disappeared inside a store nearby. She re-emerged a short time later, and in her trademark casual way, merged easily back into the crowds of shoppers and sightseers.

Suzuki crossed the street and stepped up to the window of the Kanpō Satsuma medicine store. She pushed on the door, which set a small bell jingling, and entered. Aromas of spices and herbs filled her nostrils, and while not unpleasant, again reminded her of a school science lab. It was a small shop, uncluttered, and from behind its counter an elderly man in a batik shirt stood watching her approach through horn-rimmed glasses.

'Do you treat skin problems?' she asked.

'What kind?' he asked.

'Acne.'

He turned to the wall of miniature drawers behind him, ran his finger down the labels of faded characters and pulled on a drawer handle.

'*Dokudami*,' he said, spooning a tiny sample of dried brown leaves on to some wax paper. 'Add hot water, drink as a tonic.'

'I thought dokudami was a weed?' she said, holding the sample to her nose and sniffing.

'It's cheap like weed.'

'Got anything else?'

He looked thoughtful. From another drawer he pulled a vial of white powder and placed it on the counter.

'Add this to moisturizing cream, cleanser, or lotion, once daily.'

'What is it?' she said, holding the glass tube up to the light.

'Akoya.'

'Pearl?'

'Pearl powder.'

'How much?'

'Eight thousand yen.'

'Eight thousand!'

'Why do you think I offered dokudami?'

'Why so expensive?'

'Specialty medicine. Won't find a gram under a thousand yen anywhere else. Eight thousand yen gets you a twenty per cent discount.'

She turned the vial slowly, noting the dull white colour of the contents, its icing sugar consistency. 'Who buys this stuff?' she asked.

'The Chinese. Off the cruise ships….'

'Yes, yes, I know. Where do *you* get it from?'

He peered over his horn rims and his smile disappeared.

'If you are thinking of going into business—don't. There are cheaper and more popular medicines out there. Pearl powder is not one of them.'

* * *

There was no proof that Ogino had ever used pearl powder—and it seemed unlikely that a woman who handled pearls every day for a living would spend eight thousand yen to buy her company's own product. But how could the transformation in her appearance be explained? Quite easily, Teizo might have

suggested: modern medicines were effective in treating all kinds
of skin conditions, and there was no shortage of cold creams
and steroid ointments one could get from doctors nowadays.
But what if a severe acne sufferer had tried them all, and to no
effect? What if such medicines caused allergic reactions? What
if someone was so desperate to find a cure for a debilitating
condition that they were prepared to steal for it? The questions
came thick and fast as Suzuki made her way along the esplanade
towards the hotel the next morning to cover for an ill co-worker.

At lunch time, she joined her colleagues in the cafeteria
for a bento box meal and green tea. But while the other staff
chatted about the day's strange house guests, next summer's
fashions, and the current Korean TV dramas, Suzuki's thoughts
were elsewhere. That was, until the woman beside her gave a
sudden cry and clutched at her throat.

'What's happening?' one of the staff cried and gave the
choking woman several firm slaps on the back.

'Swallowed a plum stone,' the woman said, coughing. They
rubbed her back and someone remarked, 'Don't worry, it'll
come out in your poo.' This caused the other staff to erupt in
guffaws. But Suzuki wasn't laughing; she was deep in thought.

* * *

That evening, with her mother at calligraphy class and her
daughter storied-out and purring quietly in the next room,
Suzuki poured herself a long shot of Suntory Black Label, added
ice and soda, and set herself down at the kitchen table. She
opened her laptop and inserted Danno's USB. Eight hours of
CCTV-viewing was out of the question with a bottle of whisky
in front of her. But she knew what she was looking for, and
intuition told her she would most probably find it in the post-
lunch-break hours. She fast-forwarded to 1.30 p.m., just as
D Section were returning from their meal break and watched

as each grader took their seat and resumed the mundane job of classifying pearls. Ogino seated herself at a window-side terminal and got to work typing. This scene continued unchanged for quite some time. Suzuki yawned, thankful that her own job allowed her to converse with people from all walks of life, and that no two days behind the reception desk of an international five-star hotel were ever the same.

She poured herself another glass of whisky, tempering it with soda, and fast-forwarded the player to 3.30 p.m. It was then that something curious happened. As D Section's tea break began and the staff filed out of the room, Ogino lingered. She remained at her workstation, swivelling her chair away from the ceiling camera. She then made a series of short upwards movements with her hand—not once, but half a dozen times. Suzuki peered closer at the grainy image on her monitor, not exactly sure what she had just witnessed. She rewound and viewed it again, slowing the film and noting that Ogino's movements were both swift and deliberate. She paused the player, froze the frame, and zoomed in on her reflection in the window. She clicked 'save' and transferred the image to her desktop. She then resumed the video, watching curiously as Ogino turned back to her desk, lifted a drink bottle and took several sips off it. Suzuki reached for her own glass, saw that it was empty and splashed in some more whisky. She swallowed the shot whole.

* * *

Suzuki awoke early, a hangover threatening but not enough to bring on grumpiness. She prepared breakfast—a chore she performed on weekends to give her mother a break from feeding them before work and school. Then grandmother, daughter, and granddaughter caught the train to the harbour-side Mosaic Shopping Mall to hunt for summer clothes. June to August were months Suzuki detested most. The crushing humidity, sleepless nights, and the general irritability of the Kobe populace, made the detective business less a test of acuity than one of mental and physical endurance.

After a cheap lunch at a family restaurant, they took a stroll along the harbour-front, passing knots of high school lovebirds, wedding-goers dressed in their finest, and Chinese-speaking tourists, all of whom made the esplanade the best place for people-watching in the city.

Teizo stood among the weekend fishers, a bucket beside him and his suntanned head wrapped in a small knotted white towel. The three women gathered around to inspect the wriggling rockfish that he held up, much to the delight of Suzuki's daughter.

'Any luck?' he asked Suzuki.

'Some,' she replied, then turned to her mother, asking her to buy ice cream for the four of them at the ferry terminal kiosk. As soon as they'd gone, she said, 'I'm almost certain I know who it is and how they're doing it. I just don't think this person is doing it for the money. I mean, for personal gain.'

'Motives usually make the least sense. Remember that shoplifter? Eighty-five years old. He didn't need a can of corn. All he wanted was someone to notice him ... to talk to.'

Grandmother and granddaughter returned with the ice cream, and for a moment the only sounds were of the four of them licking and lapping at the fast-melting soft cream. Later, as the three women walked back along the esplanade to the train station, Suzuki's mother nudged her shoulder. 'He's my type,' she said.

'Everyone's your type,' Suzuki said, and the two of them burst into laughter.

* * *

Sunday evening was the one time in the week when the general populace, having slept, shopped and supped, spent the dying hours of their weekend at home watching TV or preparing for Monday's onslaught. It was the perfect time to cold call.

Wearing navy blue business pants and a crisp white shirt, Suzuki stepped from the train at Suma Beach Station and re-checked the address in her notebook. The sun had dipped below the suspension bridge that connected Awaji Island to Honshu, and only the highest buildings on the hillsides now caught the last rays of golden light. Once a fishing village, Suma had long since been swallowed by Kobe's westward sprawl, and as such, one had to follow the same confounding system of numbered districts and blocks to locate a business or private residence. Here, one gave directions using local landmarks, and when this failed, they stepped on to the street to meet visitors or delivery persons. Suzuki expected no such courtesy—canniness and gut-feelings were a private detective's best friends.

It was dusk when she reached a small park on top of the hillside. A swing, slide, and sandbox strewn with forgotten plastic toys marked it as a place for daytime activity. But the aromas of curry-rice and okonomiyaki that now carried forth in the evening breeze, said life had moved elsewhere.

Suzuki felt a pang of nervousness. Confronting suspects was not her strong card, and it rarely happened. It could also be deemed illegal if a formal complaint of 'public nuisance' or stalking were made against her to the police by the suspect. But when she felt something amiss, something that couldn't be explained, or when clarity could only come from a face-to-face encounter, she would have to make her move tactfully. There was risk in this, to be sure. But Suzuki picked her battles carefully and always abided by the mantra, 'fear the person who has nothing to lose.' Ogino did not seem like such a person.

She descended the lee of the hill, through neighbourhoods that were older and more densely packed than the sea-facing side, crowded with young families, factory workers, university students, and the elderly, much like Suzuki's own.

Presently, a monument to brown stucco and Seventies-era imagination, appeared. Whoever had named the apartment building 'Laguna Heights' had had high hopes and a low budget. Suzuki stepped into the foyer and scanned its mailboxes. The names ran in vertical rows, typed except for one at the very top—No. 411. Someone had neatly written the name 'OGINO' in black marker pen.

She took the lift, still unsure of what she was about to do, or say, until she reached the fourth-floor landing. She counted off the numbers, making her way along a shared landing, cluttered with pot plants and children's bicycles, until she reached No. 411 at the very end. The door mat said 'Welcome' in five languages. She inhaled deeply, then pushed the buzzer. Moments passed. She pressed again. The door opened and a woman about the same age as her mother peered out.

'Good evening,' Suzuki said. 'May I speak to Ms Reiko Ogino, please?'

The old woman stared back at her for such a while that Suzuki wondered if she might be hard of hearing.

'May I ask who you are?' the woman said at last.

'My name is Mami Suzuki.' Then, knowing that one's company or organization name carried more weight, added, 'Of Tokai Pearls Limited.'

The name seemed to register in the old woman's gaze. 'Wait a moment, please,' she said and retreated along a dimly lit hallway. Suzuki peered into the foyer, noted the assortment of keys, good luck charms, and the seaweed green scent bottles placed on top of the shoe shelf, just like in her own foyer. Murmured voices sounded in a room down the hallway, and soon, into the light stepped Reiko Ogino.

Suzuki sensed her tension; gone was the easy gait and confident smile she had witnessed inside the Tokai Pearls building. A light frown creased Ogino's forehead, and her set jaw suggested a defensive mode.

'Yes?' she said.

'Ms Reiko Ogino?'

The woman nodded. Her frown deepened.

'My name is Mami Suzuki. I'm under contract with Tokai Pearls to investigate a certain matter regarding their stock inventory.' The formal approach always gave a suspect time to gather their thoughts; it was a technique that afforded both investigator and suspect a little breathing space, a moment to mutually assess the situation.

'I'm sorry, what exactly do you want?'

'I'd like to ask you some questions about the theft of pearls from the company.'

Ogino placed a hand on the shoe shelf. She was about to open her mouth when a soft thumping noise sounded along the hallway. A small child, a boy, appeared wearing Disney pyjamas beside her. He gripped his mother's leg and stared up at Suzuki with unabashed curiosity.

'What a cutie!' said Suzuki quickly, stepping forward and bending down. 'I love your Mickey jim-jams.'

Ogino shifted uncomfortably. She whispered something to the boy and called out to the older woman, who soon appeared and led the boy back off into the dim hallway.

'He's a nice-looking kid,' said Suzuki. 'How old?'

'Four.'

'Same as my daughter.'

Ogino didn't smile. 'I'm sorry to hear there's been a theft,' she said. 'But I can't help you. All my employees are good women. I trust them. They wouldn't steal from the company—'

'I'm not here to ask about your colleagues.'

Ogino's eyes hardened. Her jaw muscles tightened. Somewhere along the landing a home audio system was playing Queen's 'I Want to Break Free'.

'Would you mind if I came in?' Suzuki said.

'Yes, I would. I'm busy right now—perhaps another time....'

'To tell the truth, there may not be another time.' Suzuki's gaze turned solid; her tone lost its fizz. She was now all business. Ogino sensed the new atmosphere—her eyelids flitted and she wavered a moment. She reached down and drew out a pair of guest slippers, placed them on the carpet in front of Suzuki.

'My house is a mess. I apologize.'

'Don't. It can't be any worse than mine.'

Suzuki stepped into the slippers and followed Ogino into the living room. It was filled with laundered but yet-to-be-folded clothes, child's toys, a small flat-screen TV playing cartoons on low volume, and a beer can on the side table. Ogino led her to the kitchen where the dishes from the evening's dinner of curry-rice had been stacked and awaited washing.

'Please, take a seat,' Ogino said. 'You want something to drink?'

'I'll have what you're having.'

Ogino reached for a glass and a jug of barley tea from the counter.

'Beer—if you have it,' Suzuki said quickly.

Ogino gave a look of surprise, then shrugged. 'Sure.' She crossed to the fridge and pulled out a can of low-malt beer.

'Sorry, there are no clean glasses.'

'Don't worry, I never use one. Saves washing.'

Ogino gestured to a seat at the table. Suzuki sat down and placed her handbag on the floor beside her. She heard the old lady singing a lullaby in the room adjacent and the squeal of the youngster being settled.

She took the beer but waited until Ogino had returned from the lounge room with her own half-finished drink, before opening it. They sat at the table and sipped in silence.

'It's like this,' said Suzuki after a while. 'I'm a private eye, a detective—it's what I do. I have a daughter and mother to take care of just like you. So, let's be perfectly clear, this is nothing personal.'

'You're married?'

'Was.'

'Me too.'

Suzuki glanced about the small apartment. There was nothing to suggest a man had ever set foot inside—just like her own apartment.

'Well, now with the pleasantries over, I must ask some tough questions.'

'Go ahead,' said Ogino.

'Are you aware of any theft of pearls from your company?'

'No.'

'You're certain?'

Ogino nodded.

Suzuki pulled from her handbag a copy of a profile photo and pushed it across the table. 'I have reason to believe that this woman is stealing from your company.'

Ogino glanced at the picture and her eyes widened. 'That's not possible!'

'I have evidence to suggest otherwise. I will be presenting it to the company president tomorrow morning.'

'What evidence?'

'I cannot divulge that.'

Ogino looked pained.

'I know Sanae Mori very well, she's a hard worker, a good worker….' She looked at the photo, then back at Suzuki. There was desperation in her eyes. 'She's not a thief!'

'How do you know?'

'She's my niece!' Her eyes were glistening, and Suzuki knew what was about to come.

Ogino's lip began to quiver. Soon tears streamed down her smooth cheeks. In an unsteady voice, she said, 'She would never steal … it's not her.'

'It's you—isn't it?' said Suzuki.

Ogino shook her head and droplets splashed to the table top. Her strength drained, her confidence melted. She grabbed at the tissue box and blew her nose.

Suzuki began, 'You aren't greedy. You take only a half-dozen at a time, and I doubt these are what the gemologists on the sixth-floor would call "flawless beauties". After teatime, several days a week, you wait until all the employees have left the room. Then you swallow the pearls. God knows how you manage the next stage of the process—I hope you wash them well because I bought your powder from the Kanpō Satsuma medicine store the other day. Then, somehow you grind the pearls and put the powder into vials which you deliver to the old man in Chinatown. Correct?'

Ogino sniffled and took another tissue. She said nothing.

Suzuki continued, 'What I would like to know is this: why are you risking your job, your family, and your future, to steal from a company that pays you a reasonable salary?'

'Because it's not enough,' Ogino said.

'You gamble?'

Ogino shook her head.

'Alcoholic?'

'Not yet....'

'Then why?'

'Because I can't afford to support my child and my mother on a single salary. My mother is getting senile. I send her to day-care five days a week....' She began to cry without restraint, a wholehearted weeping that filled the small kitchen with sorrow.

Suzuki leant back in her chair and breathed out. She felt the weight of the woman's worries, her desperation, her responsibility as a mother and daughter, and above all, her commitment to keeping them schooled, cared-for, housed, and fed. It was an immense weight. She thought of the Mie 'sea women' searching the cold depths for pearls, for abalone, for food ... unable to breathe, unable to see the light until they reached the surface. She picked up her beer and drank it slowly. She felt like crying herself.

Ogino wiped her eyes. Her head now bowed in shame, she said nothing. She did not touch her drink.

'Do you mind if I have another beer?' Suzuki said.

Ogino looked up.

'Sorry to ask.' Suzuki smiled weakly. 'It's just that I find this job rather stressful sometimes.'

'What are you going to do?' Ogino said.

'Honestly? I'd like to get drunk.'

'I mean tomorrow, when you meet the president?'

It was the first time as a private eye that Suzuki felt the surreal quality of a moment. Here she sat, a divorced woman with a daughter and aged mother to care for, face to face with a woman of similar age, status and predicament, whose fate now rested in her hands!

Suzuki reached across the table and took Ogino's quivering hand. She felt its moist warmth and weariness. She gripped it firmly, and in a low and tender tone said, 'Let's just have another beer, shall we?'

* * *

Suzuki sat on the leather chair with her handbag resting on her lap. She was wearing a smart blue suit with an apricot blouse and camel-brown d'Orsay pumps. Through the window she glimpsed the honeycombed grey suburbs of Kobe creeping up the Rokko mountainside; so near, and yet so far.

Her gaze returned, as it had done on her first visit, to the photograph of the solo female diver on the wall before her. Around her waist a rope was tied so should she encounter difficulties, she could be pulled quickly to the surface. Sometimes, the rope snagged or got entangled and the diver would drown. Her body would be pulled to the surface limp and pale. Slavery it was not, Suzuki had learnt; the 'sea women' of Mie were proud of their ability to swim to such great depths and stay under for so long. Theirs was a sisterhood from which one could opt out at any time—but no one did.

The president cleared his throat.

'Firstly, let me convey to you my gratitude, Ms Suzuki. We are very grateful for the subtle and unobtrusive way in which you have conducted your investigation. Mr Danno, here, has told me you have some information for us. Is that correct?'

Suzuki cleared her own throat and moved to the edge of the chair. She opened her purse and took out the USB and the CCTV files, which she placed carefully on the glass coffee table in front of her.

'Thank you for requesting my services and for the generous advance payment. I am very grateful. After reviewing the staff files, the closed-circuit video footage, inspecting the grader's work environment, as well as undertaking my own fieldwork,

I must report that I can find no one who fits the profile of a thief in your company.' She threw a glance towards Danno. 'In fact, I can find no evidence that there has ever been a theft.'

The room fell silent. The president's face was unreadable, and Suzuki could not tell if her comments had pleased— or displeased him. Without a word, he rose from his chair and walked to the window. He took a moment to consider the harbour before him: the shipyards and submarine docks, the shopping mall and ferry terminal, and finally the city and the mountains beyond. He nodded to his own thoughts.

'Thank you, Ms Suzuki,' he said, turning to face her. 'The pearl industry is filled with insidious and opportunistic characters, and although they make our lives more challenging, they also ensure our wits remain sharp. It is the key to running a successful pearl trading business. You have brought me peace of mind, and I'm only sorry that I couldn't have paid you more. Nevertheless, my sincere thanks to you for your efforts.'

Suzuki gave a short, reverent bow. She thanked him once again, and sensing the meeting had ended, rose slowly from her seat. Danno moved quickly to the door and held it open. 'We have arranged a taxi for you, Ms Suzuki. Would you let me escort you to the lobby?'

As the lift descended, he said in a surprisingly casual tone, 'He does this now and again.'

'Does what?'

'Calls an investigation. It's his way of seeking assurance.'

'Assurance that he is not being stolen from?'

'It wouldn't make much difference if someone were stealing a few pearls. We have the market share in Japan and our profits are rising. No—this is personal. He thinks the theft of his pearls is theft of his soul. You see, he *is* Tokai Pearls and Tokai Pearls is him.'

'Fear blows wind in your sails, they say.'

Danno cast her a quizzical look.

'It's an old proverb,' she said. 'Fear calls us to action ... whether that fear is founded or unfounded.'

The lift doors opened, and a black taxi stood gleaming in the sunlight.

'You may be right, Ms Suzuki. Again, thank you.'

As the taxi pulled away from the lobby and passed out through the gates, she glanced back to see Danno still standing on the steps. He gave a quick, formal bow and returned inside. From a third-floor window, another face watched her depart. It was one that Suzuki had come to know well, one with whom she had shared her own worries and fears. She realized that she wasn't the only one riding life's ups and downs; sisterhood came in all shapes and forms.

Suzuki gave a short bow towards the window and the face disappeared.

* * *

The *Haru-ichiban* was still blowing the next evening as Suzuki entered the alley off Nankin-machi Street. She looked forward to Tuesday nights. With Monday blues banished, one could face the rest of the week with confidence and resolve, with a bottle of wine to help things along. The mood inside Bar Bon Voyage was thus, where customers engaged in quiet conversation over beer and wine at tables scattered about the low-lit room.

Teizo sat in his usual place at the end of the counter. He had told her once that it was a habit born of his samurai heritage, that no one, be they assassins or beautiful women, would ever escape his attention from such a vantage point.

'Case solved,' she said, sliding into the chair beside him. Her knee pressed against his.

'I'll buy you a drink,' he said.

'No, no. This one's on me. As a thanks.'

'For what?'

'For enlightening me on male fears and mermaid tears.'

She ordered a chilled bottle of Chablis and poured two glasses to their high-tide mark. As they drank, she told him the story, ending it with how she'd offered Ogino extra work by way of room cleaning at the hotel if she could manage it.

Teizo listened patiently, sipping his wine, helping the tide run out. 'How did she grind them?' he asked.

'Coffee mill.'

He chuckled. 'I'd never have thought of that.'

'That's because you're a man.'

'A man whose only fear is being rejected by a beautiful woman.'

Suzuki smiled. She glanced at her reflection in the mirrored glass of the bar and said, 'You were right about that pearl powder though … it does work.'

Land of the Gods

Autumn was Suzuki's favourite season. It was when the ginkgo trees shed their gold across the city sidewalks, persimmons were sold for a song in the wholesale markets, and the burnished copper hues of the hillsides made the Rokko mountains a sight to behold. It was also the one time of the year when the briny breath of the harbour bowed to the sweet fragrance of the orange olive blossom drifting from the small parks and gardens behind the quays.

The November morning had dawned cool and clear. By 8.30 a.m. she was in uniform and managing the check-out traffic behind the long cedar desk of the Orient Hotel. Tsuro, the night-shift manager, handed her an envelope on his way out. 'Delivered this morning,' he said, 'enjoy your day'.

Pondering the crisp washi paper with the Tokai Pearls Limited insignia, her first thought was of the paranoid company president requesting her services yet again. Instead, the letter revealed the sender to be his right-hand man, Danno.

It was a request to meet, not with him, but with a female acquaintance. The missive was brief: Ms Rumi Shimizu had a personal matter that she would like to discuss in confidence. There was a phone number penned below. For a young man, Danno displayed eccentric old-school thinking, Suzuki thought.

A handwritten letter could not be hacked, accidentally deleted, or be waylaid in a spam folder. Moreover, it demanded an immediate reply.

Kobe's private investigators, at least the good ones, rarely advertised. Word of mouth travelled as swiftly as the *Haru-ichiban* through the city's alleyways and avenues, generating more business than a hundred hand-delivered mailbox leaflets could ever do. It was a system of trust and mutual benefit, whereupon a private eye, in return for their modest fee, provided a client with services that were timely, professional, and discreet—'discretion' being the optimal word here, because to approach the Kobe Metropolitan Police was to wade into a quagmire of paperwork, uncomfortable questions, and worst of all, the risk of a private matter being made public.

She waited until her tea break to step from the hotel and cross the esplanade to the harbour-side. Save for a pair of teenage lovebirds cuddling beside the old lighthouse and a fisherman casting into the slack tide, the quay was quiet.

She glanced back at the hotel. There was risk in moonlighting. Should management discover her sleuth-for-hire sideline, she might lose her job. It was less a case of 'double-dipping' than of showing disloyalty to one's company, even if the salary she received wasn't enough to cover childcare, aged-care, and all the other bills in between. The irony was thus: that in order to uncover others' secrets, she must carefully guard her own.

She slipped Danno's note from her waistcoat pocket, inputted the phone number and let the dial tone run. A voice messaging service sounded. She terminated the call and was about to return to the hotel when her phone vibrated.

The caller's voice was cool—the words clipped—as if caught at an inopportune time. At the mention of Danno, however, it warmed.

'Thank you so much for calling, Ms Suzuki. To be honest I didn't expect a reply. I mean, you must be….' A pause. 'Would you be available to meet tomorrow?'

'I'm free from eight in the evening, if that suits?'

'Do you know the Nishimura Coffee Shop?'

To not know the old dame of Kobe's coffee-house world was to be either a tourist or a tea drinker. Recently, its popularity had overtaken its prestige, and there were now several branches across the city.

'May I ask which one?' said Suzuki.

'Kitanozaka?'

'I'll be wearing a blue suit and carrying a beige attaché case.' She signed off with a thank you and goodbye. Small talk was best kept for face-to-face encounters.

She returned to the hotel reception, swallowed a cup of green tea, and set to task with yet another mundane case of hotel detective work: an elderly guest had mislaid her Louis Vuitton parasol somewhere in the lobby.

* * *

The next evening, dressed in her Aoyama pantsuit of royal navy and a crisp white shirt with an open collar, she placed her attaché case in her bicycle basket, and careful not to scrape her brown Diana pumps, coasted downhill to the train station. It was a short ride to Sannomiya followed by a brisk walk up the incline to Kitano district.

Beneath the glow of Taisho-era streetlamps, she moved easily through the dinner crowds along Kitanozaka Street. She passed by Kokubu, the inexpensive wagyu beef restaurant she knew and loved, and realized with surprise that two years to this very day, she had treated her mother and daughter to a steak dinner in celebration of receiving a *tantei-gyo no todokede*, her private investigator's licence. For all its usual bureaucratic bother, City Hall had only wanted proof that she had no prior convictions, was neither a crime syndicate member, nor a person of 'unsound mind'. The process, like Kokubu's well-oiled teppan, had been wonderfully smooth.

The Nishimura Coffee Shop lay at the end of the street. On sighting its faux Tudor façade and lamp-lit windows, she felt another twinge of nostalgia. As a child she'd accompanied her grandmother on Sunday shopping expeditions, ending them over a towering parfait at one of Nishimura's first-floor alcove tables.

On entering, Suzuki's gaze roamed the large low-lit salon. Finding none of its tables occupied by a solo female customer, she was about to take the stairs to the second level when a sudden movement caught her eye. A woman rose from a table half-hidden by a potted palm on the far side of the room. Beside her sat a young man and a girl.

Suzuki smiled.

She made her way between the tables of coffee-drinkers, noting all she could about the three people ahead of her without staring.

Rumi Shimizu cut a slim, elegant figure in long beige slacks, a cream cashmere sweater, and a tailored brown suede jacket. She was tall and wore her dyed chestnut hair up, sculpted against her head in the style favoured by Kobe's executive women. The young man was similarly tall, had high cheekbones and wore the loose, casual clothes of a university student. The girl, dressed in the maroon-and-grey uniform of Kobe Municipal Fukiai Girls High School, watched curiously as Suzuki approached them.

'Thank you so much for coming at such short notice, Ms Suzuki,' Rumi Shimizu said, stepping forward. She motioned to a corner chair. 'Please sit with us.'

With the young man beside her and the two women facing her, the configuration reminded Suzuki of an old-fashioned railway car but with the atmosphere of a job interview.

A waitress attired in a French maid uniform appeared and took their orders. Suzuki, sensing awkwardness, remarked on the sudden coolness of the weather. They nodded and replied with a 'yes'.

Then, they waited.

The coffee arrived, dark and steaming, in four bone china cups. Suzuki did not touch her cup until Rumi Shimizu had taken her first sip. The moments before a potential client revealed their problem were the most suspenseful—often more so than the investigation itself. There was no point in speculating, such was the variety of cases Suzuki had encountered over the past two years: a gambling-addicted spouse, an insurance fraudster, a cheating fiancé, a geriatric shoplifter, a bus driver with an underwear fetish, a pearl thief … no two cases were ever alike.

'My husband,' said Rumi Shimizu in a lowered voice. She glanced furtively at the young man and girl. '*Their* father has disappeared.'

Suzuki sat with her back straight, her hands resting in her lap. Her senses keenly tuned to voice tone, facial muscles, eye movements—anything that might help her gauge the nature of the situation and the trustworthiness of her potential client. Because until she possessed all details, that's all they were—potential.

Rumi Shimizu took out a photograph from her purse and placed it on the table in front of Suzuki. It was a family snapshot taken with an SLR camera and printed on Fujifilm colour paper. The occasion was *Hatsumode*, the ritual New Year's visit to a Shinto shrine to pray for health, wealth, and happiness.

'My husband's name is Yukihiro. We celebrated his fifty-sixth birthday last Monday, without him.'

The daughter bowed her head and began to sob.

Suzuki lifted the photo and held it to the light. Shimizu was a tall, heavy-set man, with a face younger than his fifty-six years. She noted his set jaw, dark cropped hair, sparkling eyes, and awkward grin. It was the self-conscious smile of a person who disliked having their photo taken by a passing stranger. She knew that feeling well.

'He's been gone for almost two weeks now,' Rumi Shimizu said. 'We wish to seek your help in finding him.'

Suzuki laid the photo on the table. That the Shimizu family sat before her now meant two things: that Yukihiro Shimizu's disappearance was out of character and that the Kobe Metropolitan Police had not been contacted.

Men, women, and children disappeared every day across Japan. A domestic situation usually resolved itself, with the spurned family member returning regretful and apologetic sooner or later. Others ended less happily. That 17 out of every 100,000 citizens took their lives each year was no small number in a land of 120 million precious souls. Abductions and murders were less common, but even they stood a higher chance of being solved because of public and governmental pressure on the police.

She took out her notebook and pen. She began with the easy questions, scribbling down Rumi Shimizu's answers, which came quietly and softly. Her husband had left for work in the predawn hours of Friday, 22 October. He had cycled to Shinkaichi Station, from where he took the subway train to Kobe Station before making the short walk to Mikuni Hotel, which stood at the other end of the harbour, facing the Orient

Hotel. Only, that morning he never arrived. His bicycle was found locked inside the Shinkaichi Station parking lot.

'To confirm—the police aren't involved?' Suzuki asked.

Rumi Shimizu shook her head.

'Any reason to believe he may have left under duress?'

'What do you mean?'

'Did he seem bothered, upset, or stressed?'

'Not that I noticed.' She looked at her children. Their faces concurred.

'Okay—let's return to that one later. What does he do?'

'He's the hotel's head chef.'

'At Uoshin, the seafood restaurant?'

'He's worked there for almost fifteen years.' Rumi Shimizu took a sip of her coffee and returned the cup to its saucer with a clatter. 'He took an overnight bag. Clothes were gone from his drawers and wardrobe.'

'What kind of clothes?'

'Casual, autumn weight, nothing flashy.'

'Any bank withdrawals?'

'We share an account—his salary is paid into it—but it hasn't been touched.'

'What about Uoshin? What did management say?'

'They're as confused as I am. He was supposed to receive an award for gourmet excellence from the City of Kobe a week after he disappeared.'

Suzuki's pen worked quickly across the page. 'Anything else?'

'His knives are missing.'

She glanced up. 'How many knives are we talking about?'

'I'm not sure … I can find out.'

'Perhaps this will be of help,' said the son with a suddenness that startled Suzuki. Far from meek, his voice was mature and calm. He held an envelope out to her. She looked at Rumi Shimizu, who said quickly, 'It was addressed to my son and daughter. Please, go ahead.'

Suzuki slipped out the letter and read.

To Sota and Miku,
Please forgive me. I promised to take you both fishing on Awaji Island—I am sorry.
Papa

The kanji and kana characters were written in a fluid yet precise hand. That his wife's name appeared nowhere on the paper seemed curious. Even more so was the postal stamp: issued by Matsue General Post Office on 23 October.

Suzuki frowned. 'Shimane Prefecture?'

'Kobe is his hometown,' said Rumi Shimizu. 'Shimane was where he attended university.'

'How long ago?'

'About thirty-five years....'

'What did he major in?'

'Medical technology, I think. He wanted to work in a hospital.'

Suzuki turned these details over in her mind. A medical technician and a sushi chef were not necessarily incongruous professions if one considered that both required precision tools and a high degree of skill to use them.

'Do you mind if I photograph this?' she asked.

'By all means.'

Suzuki slipped out her phone, took several snapshots, and returned the letter to its envelope. She picked up her cup and drained it. Looking thoughtful, she said, 'I might just order another.'

Rumi Shimizu managed a weak smile. 'Then I will, too.'

Over the steaming rim of her second cup, Suzuki considered what she had gleaned so far: Shimane Prefecture, an apology letter to the children and not the wife, missing knives, a prestigious restaurant without its master chef, and a family without its father. She put down her cup and gazed at the faces before her. Three meditating monks could have offered her more meaningful body language.

'In your collective opinion, why do *you* think he disappeared?' she asked.

A moment passed. When Rumi Shimizu finally spoke, Suzuki assumed it was for all of them.

'All we want is to find him. We want him home.'

Suzuki glanced about the salon, at the fashionable women photographing their desserts, the elderly newspaper readers in their shoe-string neckties, and the young couples flitting between parfaits and profiteroles. The levity of their behaviour suddenly irritated her. She took a deep breath. It was time for the difficult questions.

These she addressed to Rumi Shimizu directly. Did her husband have any mental or physical health problems? Secret debts? A mistress? A boyfriend? Had there been any family issues? Arguments? Grudges? Problems at work?

Almost all investigations began in complete darkness. Then, piece-by-piece, drip-by-drip, information illuminated a path forward. But Rumi Shimizu's answers yielded not even a spark.

Suzuki felt the cold creep of desperation. She needed more details; she needed more because she needed the job. Her mother's eye surgery scheduled for next month would be expensive and her National Health Insurance would cover only two-thirds of the cost. She changed her tactics. 'May I ask what all of you do?'

'Sota is a student at Kwansei Gakuin University in Nishinomiya. Miku is a second-year high school student in Kobe. I work for Tiffany.'

'Tiffany & Co. The jewellery company?'

'I'm the purchasing manager at the Sannomiya branch.'

Suzuki felt a neuron flash behind her eyeballs. The Danno connection? She filed it away.

There was no point in probing for more. She now turned to the subject of payment for services rendered. It was a formality, but one which she felt least adequate discussing. To be sure, clients with pressing personal problems were unlikely to shop around for the best deal in private eyes. The Shimizu family didn't strike her as being poor or picky—just unfortunate—and it was this point that gnawed at her. Was she benefiting from others' misfortunes? Or, was she helping solve their problems and, dare she say it, make the world a better place? It was a two-headed beast her conscience had yet to tame.

She took out a printed schedule of fees from her attaché case and handed it to Rumi Shimizu; the bottom line—half up front, half on completion, with expenses paid in full, regardless of the outcome of the investigation.

'Then you'll help us?' the son said, his tone earnest.

She levelled her gaze on his and said, 'Let's just consider what we've shared today, and we'll talk again tomorrow, shall we?'

'Mr Danno was right,' said the daughter.

'Pardon me?'

'You're both professional ... *and* cool.'

Suzuki flushed. She would take 'professional' any day, but 'cool' wasn't a term she'd have thought synonymous with a forty-year-old single mother who treasured her tracksuit pants and drank a little too much beer on weeknights. 'Thank you,' she replied, and searched for her wallet.

Rumi Shimizu rose from her seat, politely refusing payment for the coffee. 'Thank you, Ms Suzuki. We appreciate you meeting with us this evening.'

The three family members stood and bowed solemnly. They were still standing when she pushed through Nishimura's heavy oak doors and stepped out into the cool autumn night.

* * *

Rain had dampened Kitanozaka Street. The air, though refreshing, did nothing for her headache as she descended the incline to Sannomiya Station.

Shimane Prefecture.

The name troubled her. What did she know about Shimane? Except that it was a rural backwater with the second-lowest population of Japan's forty-seven prefectures. High school geography classes had seared into her mind images of craggy seashores and forlorn fishing villages, of a hinterland scarred by dormant volcanoes, plunging valleys, and raging rivers. Nightmarish geography to a private investigator. She carried her frown all the way to the station.

Aboard the train, she recalled her first missing-persons case two years ago when the parents of a middle-school student had contacted her. It hadn't been a particularly difficult assignment; she had merely talked to the girl's friends and soon after found her sleeping at a 24-hour Internet cafe in a neighbouring town. Over hot milk tea, she had listened to the teenager's fears of failing her high school entrance exam and consoled and encouraged her to contact her worried parents.

Adults were different.

They were capable of much greater range and self-concealment. The most difficult of all cases were those where the 'missing' chose not to be found. They even had their own terminology: *johatsu*—'evaporation' cases. Most private investigators refused them for lack of concrete details and the slim chance of success.

Suzuki watched the stations come and go, peering down at the microcosms of life which clustered about neon-lit entrances and forecourts, and lively standing-drink shops, noodle joints, and red lantern pubs with their smoking braziers and crowded counters. Amidst the urban crush, anyone could hide in plain sight with relative ease. Big cities *made* people anonymous.

On the face of it, Yukihiro Shimizu seemed like a good father and loyal husband. Rumi Shimizu had spoken of his long working hours and of his rare days off on which he took Sota and Miku on fishing trips to Suma Beach. One day, a quiet, hard-working family man—the next, an empty chair at the dining table and a sushi counter without its master chef.

She considered the restaurant connection. Uoshin ranked as one of Kobe's finest seafood establishments—if not, its most infamous. A decade ago, it had been the scene of a botched yakuza assassination attempt in which a doctor had accidentally been shot dead. That alone, not to mention its menu of the potentially lethal puffer fish cuisine, made Uoshin a must-visit for thrill-seeking gourmands. Given this reputation and the handsome salary an upper-tier employee would command, it didn't seem to her like a position one would vacate easily.

Or, did it?

She reined in her thoughts, reminding herself that while the reasons for Yukihiro Shimizu's disappearance were important, they wouldn't necessarily lead to finding him.

The train slowed down. The conductor announced her station. When the doors opened, she stepped on to the platform with more questions than she had boarded with. Plumbing the depths of possibility and reason was now beyond her mental energy levels.

Descending the stairs, her thoughts turned to the one person whose opinion she could count on. It was true that his pearls of wisdom were sometimes a little over-lustrous on account of a brimming sake cup; however, to wage friendly battles of wit over a drink or two in his company made life bearable, even fun. Problem was, he rarely answered his phone. It made her wonder if this 'radio silence' was the ruse of an old fox; a way of forcing a rendezvous over a chilled Chablis at Bar Bon Voyage, or some other side-street pub where the lighting was kind to older men and not-so-young women.

Her headache eased.

In the bicycle parking lot, she slipped out her phone and pressed 'Teizo', resolving to break his radio silence.

* * *

Friday was the only other day of the week, besides Tuesday, that her mother could pick up her daughter from the Octopus Garden kindergarten, and when being a little heavy-handed with Chardonnay wouldn't weigh too heavily on Saturday's obligations.

At 5.30 p.m., having traded her tight-fitting uniform for boots, black jeans and a sweater of caramel cashmere, she walked out of Motomachi Station and to its bustling forecourt. Car radio rap and the rolling thunder of Kawasaki and Yamaha cruisers fought for noise superiority amidst the rush-hour traffic which swept back and forth along Motomachi Koka-Street.

Seemingly oblivious, Teizo sat thumbing a pocket novella on a bench nearby. He had on blue canvas pants and a scuffed leather jacket half-zipped against the cool evening, and his freshly cropped hair and tanned face caught the last rays of sunlight streaming between the office buildings.

'You've cut your hair,' she said.

He smiled but didn't look up. 'It was weighing on my mind.'

She guffawed. 'Well, the baseball-coach-look suits you.'

He ignored the quip, rose from the bench, and pocketed his book. 'A drink before dinner?'

'How about we cut straight to the food. I'm starving and I've got to be home by eight.'

They followed the elevated railway line, past a hole-in-the-wall tobacco store and a Kobe Metropolitan Police *koban* where bored cops lounged behind beige desks. Then, Teizo wheeled right and led her beneath the overpass. They entered a narrow alley lined with tiny shops, many no bigger than closets and cluttered with antiques and curios, handcrafted jewellery, used Americana, custom-made skateboards, and all manner of upcycled junk. There were fortune tellers, Chinese masseuses, curry stands, and bánh mì counters. Commuter trains rattled back and forth overhead making conversation pointless.

Then, in front of a noren entrance curtain daubed with the characters すし, he halted.

'Sign says they're not open till seven,' she said.

'I made a reservation.' He lifted the curtain and rolled back the door.

The restaurant's name was Sakaya. It was not so much a restaurant as a counter with seven seats. From behind the kitchen curtain came the click-clacking of wooden clogs, then a raspy voice called, 'Irasshaimase!' It belonged to an elderly man with bloodshot eyes and jowls as smooth as polished driftwood. A crisp, boat-shaped white hat perched on his nut-brown head.

On sighting Teizo, his gold tooth gleamed. 'Did it take a dinner date with a beautiful woman to remind you that you still have an uncle?'

'I've been too busy trying to catch fish to eat them,' Teizo replied, then to her, 'Uncle Masuo is my father's younger brother.'

In the twelve months she'd known him, never once had he mentioned an uncle who ran a sushi shop beneath the Motomachi train track. The old man bowed. 'Maido,' he greeted, and placed a bottle of chilled Kirin lager with two glasses before them.

Teizo poured her glass full. 'You said you wanted sushi, so I ordered ahead.'

'You're a man of great foresight,' she said.

They toasted and drank deeply, agreeing that beer tasted better in autumn.

The motion of the old chef's blade passing effortlessly through the flesh, freeing slice after slice from the glistening fillet, had an almost hypnotic effect. He worked quietly, surely—unconcerned if anyone was watching or not, and soon a sumptuous sashimi no moriawase comprising *akami* (lean dark tuna), *amadai* (tilefish), *hamachi* (yellowtail), *yoichi* (long spiked Hokkaido sea urchin), and *tsubugai* (conch shell) lay before them.

She couldn't recall her last visit to a traditional sushiya. Mostly, grandmother, mother, and daughter rode their bicycles to the nearest Sushiro restaurant chain store to gorge on plates of machine-made sushi. That the toppings were thawed and the part-time staff slow mattered little. The bill, as per the taste, was cheap.

But today, the two of them ate without haste, allowing the juices to course through their mouths and flood their senses. They poured each other's glasses, sipped, and spectated on the old chef as he turned to prepare the sushi rice; first, adding vinegar to the steaming grains, working them gently with his bamboo spatula, then shaping them with deft movements into bite-sized pieces on to which nigiri toppings were delicately affixed.

When the feasting had finished, Suzuki pulled out her notebook.

'What do Shimane Prefecture and sushi have in common?' she asked Teizo.

He drained his glass and said, 'That's like asking, what do hot springs and Nagano have in common? Or snow and Hokkaido.' He turned to his uncle. 'Ojisan, a question for you.'

At the risk of sounding foolish, she repeated herself. The old chef rinsed his hands and wiped them on a towel. He looked thoughtful, as if from many possibilities he must choose the best one. 'The freshest squid comes from the Sea of Japan. Summer is the place to eat firefly squid in Shimane.'

'And in autumn?'

'Shijimi shellfish from Lake Shinji in Matsue. The water flows in and out from the sea. It's colder now and the currents are heavier with nutrients.'

She scribbled quickly. Nothing could be discounted. When all had been left to ferment, the essence would rise to the surface. She thanked him graciously.

The old chef excused himself, asking Teizo to mind the shop while he ran an errand at the nearby liquor store.

When he'd left, she asked, 'Why would a seemingly happy family man and successful sushi chef abandon his family and run off to Shimane?'

'A missing person's case?'

'Uh-huh.'

'How do you know he was happy?'

'I'm yet to find otherwise.'

'Homelife, worklife … pressure can get to a man.'

'And not a woman?'

'What I mean is, running away can be an act of survival, an alternative to self-destruction, or worse.' He lifted the bottle and topped up their glasses. 'Why Shimane? No idea.'

'Where did you attend university?'

'Why?'

'Just tell me.'

'Fukuoka.'

'Do you ever return? You know, for nostalgic reasons?'

'Used to. To revisit our old drinking haunts. Most of them are gone now and the old boys are scattered to the wind. Those of us still alive, that is.'

His uncle returned carrying a large flagon of sake.

Her pen poised over paper, she asked, 'Apart from Izumo Taisha Shrine, what else is Shimane famous for?'

'It has the highest number of sunless days in Japan,' Teizo replied.

His uncle laughed. 'That it does!' He placed the flagon upside-down in the dispenser. 'You mentioned Izumo Taisha Shrine. Well, according to the old calendar, November is called *Kaminazuki* … when gods from all over Japan depart their home shrines to gather at Izumo Taisha.'

'That's right,' said Teizo. 'And you know what they call Shimane?'

'Land of Sunless Days?' she ventured.

'Land of the Gods,' corrected the old chef.

It was food for thought.

Though why a big city sushi chef would join the heavenly highway to Shimane in November offered no logical answer. Nevertheless, she made a note, knowing fully well that even the slightest or most seemingly trivial piece of information could ultimately be crucial to her investigation.

'Are sushi chefs spiritual?' she asked.

At first, the old chef seemed not to hear. She shot Teizo a sideways glance, wondering if she had blundered. But when his uncle spoke, the words had been carefully considered: 'Any profession that involves taking life, be it farmer, hunter, or fisherman, gives thanks to the Shinto gods.' He motioned to a small altar, perched like a swallow's nest on the wall above him. It was dedicated to Ebisu, one of the *Shichi-fuku-jin*, the Seven Gods of Luck, and patron of fishermen and tradesmen. His huge earlobes, crescent grin, a fishing rod in one hand, and a red snapper tucked under his other arm, marked him as the jolliest of the seven deities.

'Sushi chefs are gods of the culinary world—at least, the good ones are,' Teizo said. 'To become a master chef is a long journey. Years of apprenticeship, learning knife care, cutting techniques, fish quality, seasonal specialities, business skills, negotiating, networking …'

His uncle's gold tooth gleamed. 'Ha! You remember well, Teizo-kun.' He turned to her. 'When my nephew was a young man, he wanted to be a sushi chef, but his father discouraged it. He told him: it's not a job but a way of life. You must be all in, or all out—there are no two ways about it.'

Teizo's cheeks glowed.

'The master chef is first to arrive and last to leave his station,' the old man said and grinned. 'In my case, that's any time I please.'

It was a bittersweet remark. The lot of a working single mother was a dawn-till-dusk treadmill of eat, sleep, work, and care for an aged parent and young child in between. Unlike a sushi chef, she didn't have a choice.

Teizo's question of marital happiness returned to her mind. The possibility of an illicit love affair could not be discounted. All too often, they were the cause of empty marriages, and by the same token, the result of them. Rumi Shimizu hadn't made any mention of a secret romance involving her husband. Fear of public shame might have prevented her. For better or for worse, love—or the need to be loved—was a powerful catalyst of human behaviour. Her thoughts turned to the man at her side.

'Romance?' said Teizo.

She flinched. 'Romance?'

'Well, Shinto shrines and clams from Lake Shinji don't really matter if there's a romantic connection, do they?'

'Noted.' She breathed out, relieved that he hadn't read her mind.

Yet, the question of Shimizu's missing knives bothered her. It would be her final question.

The old chef glanced up from his workstation, his bloodshot gaze suddenly animated. 'You ask me, how *important* are my knives?' He looked at the tools of his trade arrayed on a pure white cloth beneath the drying lamp, lustrous and sleek as freshly landed fish. 'A chef's knife is an extension of himself.' He lifted one and sent its glimmer racing about the walls of the shop. 'The knife's edge is where his soul meets with the soul of the fish that has given its life, and so he treats both with the utmost respect.'

She thanked him for sharing his knowledge and the fine meal that he had served them. She glanced at her watch and was about to enquire of the bill, when the old chef smiled. 'It's been paid,' he told her.

Teizo stood at the door, holding it open.

* * *

At precisely 8 p.m., Suzuki's phone rang.

In the midst of helping her daughter with a Little Mermaid jigsaw puzzle, she rose from the kotatsu-heated table, and despite a chill breeze blowing off the Seto Inland Sea, stepped on to the apartment balcony and closed the door behind her.

Rumi Shimizu was polite, her voice resolute. 'My family and I would like to request your services. That is … if you are willing to help us?'

Suzuki had prepared herself for this moment. She cleared her throat. 'Thank you for your kind words, and for your interest in my services. I am happy to take your case. However, I must tell you that a trip to Shimane will be necessary and this will affect my expenses.'

There was a moment of silence and it caused Suzuki to hope, for the briefest instant, that Rumi Shimizu might refuse. A journey to Shimane would mean taking the paid day holiday she had fought hard for to attend her daughter's sports day the coming weekend. The wind now wailed in her ears. In the distance, a dinner cruiser lit as a ghost ship passed silently through the inky darkness.

'We are prepared to pay,' said Rumi Shimizu.

Suzuki stifled a shiver. 'Thank you. Then I'll leave early Friday.'

'*This* Friday?'

'*Zen wa isoge*. The sooner the better.' Before Rumi Shimizu could respond, she added, 'I'll do my best, but I must also tell you, in the event that I do find your husband, it's not in my legal capacity to make contact with him.'

A brief silence followed, then Rumi Shimizu answered, 'My family and I thank you.'

The call ended. The wind stiffened. The cruise boat had vanished behind the headland, leaving only the vague lights of distant marine traffic to say there was even a sea at all out there.

Somewhere in the cold darkness, she hoped Yukihiro Shimizu was alive and breathing. She hoped he would make life easy for her—and for his own family. To Ebisu she offered a silent prayer.

* * *

Three days later, having kissed her sleeping daughter lightly and hugged her mother, and taken a taxi to Shin-Kobe Station where she'd boarded the shinkansen at dawn, she fought off feelings of guilt at having abandoned them. Thank goodness for supportive friends. They would ensure that grandmother and daughter survived the kindergarten's annual sports day without her. She made a mental note to buy all of them thank-you gifts.

At Okayama Station, an hour's train ride west of Kobe, she transferred to the Yakumo Express, an ageing diesel-powered passenger train that made the three-hour trip five times daily across the Chūgoku Sanchi mountain range to Matsue on the Sea of Japan coast.

While its passengers dozed, read manga comics, or scrolled through baseball highlights on their phones, the passing countryside revealed itself beneath a veil of mist. No longer verdant, it stretched out on both sides in a pale patchwork of freshly shorn fields that said the rice harvest had almost ended. Thick golden sheaves hung on drying trestles. Next would come the threshing machines, followed by the bittersweet smoke of the chaff piles cloaking the land, and finally, the last of the autumn festivals would fill the air with volleys of taiko drumbeats and the chants of half-naked men carrying portable shrines through their village streets.

The train stopped to take on passengers at the canal town of Kurashiki, then swung north to join the wide slow-moving Takahashi River. The air grew silky, softening the rocky outcrops and lending the serpentine swathe a dreamlike quality as it wended back towards the Seto Inland Sea.

Soon, the Chūgoku Sanchi mountain range reared its head. The tunnels grew longer and more numerous. As the railway line pushed deeper north, migratory birds appeared on the river's sandbars, warming themselves in the sunlight; where the sun was yet to reach, hamlets came and went in the mist. The train thundered onwards, passing cow sheds with caved-in roofs, homesteads pierced by rampaging bamboo, and graveyards of rusted farm machinery—no place for youthful minds, and yet crying out for youthful energy. Who would be left to resuscitate the heartland if the big cities kept wooing its young blood? It was a question for the politicians. Suzuki had no answers.

Later, they pulled in at Bitchu village, where elderly passengers disembarked with well-worn suitcases and paper parcels, to be met by even more ancient taxi drivers who welcomed them like old friends. The train continued on its way, rattling through gorges and tunnels, and over bridges spanning foaming cataracts, which turned to emerald torrents that hurried southward.

The 'Swinging Yakumo' Teizo called it. He had warned her that it was a rail journey like none other. The nickname had sounded cute at the time. Now, as she made her way up the lurching aisle, she changed her mind. Every violent shift and jerk of the floor caused her to gasp. Between cars she leapt across scything steel plates to reach the restroom, uttering a cry loud enough to turn some passengers' heads.

It was not until they stopped in the village of Niimi to await the passing southbound train that she found a chance to safely pour a cup of roasted green tea from her flask and spread her research on the tray table.

Johatsu.

The word had grown dark from underlining. Stigma placed it in the same taboo basket as *jisatsu* (suicide), *karōshi* (death-by-overwork), and *hikikomori* (the social withdrawal phenomenon). Each year, thousands of individuals simply upped and left behind families, work responsibilities, and financial obligations, vanishing on their own accord, often with not so much as a note of explanation. Some left letters or made phone calls, which was considerate but not always helpful. Many didn't. Strict privacy laws prevented even immediate family from obtaining addresses, records of credit card use, or driver's licence renewal information—details that might otherwise help to locate them. Moreover, unless the person had committed a criminal act, nothing could be legally done to make them return. Johatsu left loved ones feeling abandoned, angry, and almost always heartbroken.

Now, as the train lurched out of Niimi, Suzuki ran her pencil beneath the question she was most reluctant to tackle: if Yukihiro Shimizu was a johatsu candidate, what had triggered it? His wife had not divulged any emotional trauma or mental health issues, but like johatsu itself, a client may be unwilling to admit to any of them.

She poured a second cup of tea and watched the vapour rise and dissipate. Confronting an emotionally unstable sushi chef with a full set of fish knives was not high on her bucket list; her job was solely to locate the missing person and inform the client. Private investigating, however, was a lot like single motherhood: it was a game of ever-changing dynamics where one had to adapt—or succumb.

Before that thought could devolve further, her senses were arrested by a peculiar sight. Beyond the window the river flowed north. With the Chūgoku Sanchi mountain range now behind them, the Land of the Gods beckoned.

* * *

Stepping on to the Matsue Station platform, a salty tang filled her nostrils, so unlike the tired potpourri of diesel fumes, industrial detergent, and tidal odours one inhaled on the Kobe harbour quays.

'Welcome to the City of Water,' announced the arrivals hall hoarding. Matsue was small for a prefectural capital; its population of 200,000 inhabitants was just an eighth of Kobe. Still, Suzuki was under no illusions; a smaller haystack did not make the needle easier to find. But standing on the station concourse, her senses tingled; something told her she had the right haystack.

At the tourist bureau opposite, she approached the charming young staff and enquired about places of interest, steering him quickly from canal and castle tours to the subject of seafood restaurants. He beamed; there were many, he said. She tightened the net. Sushi restaurants? A half-dozen reputable ones, he replied, pointing them out in a full colour brochure.

To the uninitiated, 'Matsue nightlife' might have sounded like an oxymoron. The tourism paraphernalia, however, revealed a thriving culinary scene, and it was this which caused her to sigh; slogging between six sushi restaurants would be more than enough excitement for one night in the City of Water.

After thanking the staff, she set off for her hotel. Walking kept a client's bills down. It also combined physical exercise with reconnoitring in a way that riding in a taxi could not. In a short while she reached a tree-lined canal where tour boats puttered up and down the tea green water. Crossing a stone bridge, the broadcast commentaries of their conical-hatted tiller men drifted up, curious in accent and vernacular.

A familiar aroma reached her on the canal breeze. Ranging its sides for the source, her gaze settled on a turn of the century stone building with an ivy-smothered façade and a sign outside that announced, 'coffee and club sandwiches'. Over a window table, she spread her tourist map and began cross-referencing sushi restaurants with her phone navigation. Slowly, her evening plans began to take shape.

That a big city sushi master would come to a town like Matsue and do nothing seemed illogical. Yukihiro Shimizu hadn't touched the family bank account, so unless he had met with someone—a friend, lover, or accomplice—he would need money. The missing knives came to mind. Just as a barber or a masseuse might pick up work in any village, town or city, a chef could easily do likewise without arousing suspicions.

When her sandwich and coffee arrived, she ate hungrily, resolving not to snack again until the evening. Presenting Rumi Shimizu with receipts from six sushi restaurants would require tactful explaining, but if her husband was to be discovered working at one, all would be forgiven.

Revived, she set out once more for her hotel. She'd read that American private eyes were called 'gumshoes' because their rubber soles allowed for stealthy pursuit. As she trod the uneven flagstones of the canal path, she wondered if her own pink-and-grey Asics Walkers qualified her? If the company ever produced a product called 'Asics Stealth', she would be their first customer.

In a short while, she was standing on the busy Shinjiko Bridge. She had arrived at the Ohashi River, the conduit of two great bodies of water: the Sea of Japan, which lay somewhere behind her, and Lake Shinji, whose waters now spread like a blinding plane of silver before her.

The Matsue Sunrise Hotel rose from a copse of red pines on the other side of the bridge. It was a relic from the bubble era of the 1980s—an eye-sore, to be sure. Yet, it guaranteed a panoramic view of the hotel's namesake each morning. It was also cheap.

The staff were gracious and polite, offering her an upgrade on the sixth-floor, and once inside her room, she collapsed on the bed exhausted.

She awoke in the late afternoon, alarmed at having slept for so long. She quickly drank some green tea and changed into her tracksuit pants, then she slipped into her 'gumshoes' and left the hotel.

Walking, a Buddhist priest had once told her, was meditation for people who couldn't sit still. It helped untangle the mess of thoughts and information the mind accumulated during the day. In this thinking she was not alone; a river of humanity flowed across Shinjiko Bridge, a slow-motion frenzy of homebound office workers, high schoolers, joggers, university kids, and dog walkers, but who, like herself, seemed to pause a moment to meditate on the majesty of the lake at sunset.

They hailed the great saffron disk with their phones held high—oohing and aahing—and even the taxi drivers slowed down to kindly allow their passengers to take in the moment. Suzuki stepped to the bridge rail and peered into the water. A soft gurgle drifted up as the outgoing tide pressed against the bridge pillars and ripples made by feeding fish widened across its pink surface. As the sun slipped silently into Lake Shinji, she drew a breath. The past was history, and the future was yet to happen—only the present mattered. It was less an epiphany than a reminder not to let life's simple pleasures go unappreciated. She slipped out her phone and pressed 'Home'.

'Hello?' her mother answered. 'Do you know where I keep my spare reading glasses?'

'I'm fine—and how are you?'

'I'm sorry, it's just that I've gone and lost my glasses again.'

'Are they on top of your head?'

A pause, then came a shrill laugh. 'I'm so sorry! Must have forgotten.'

'How was sports day?'

'Fine.'

'What are you doing now?'

'Cooking.'

'What's for dinner?'

'*Oden*. It's Saturday, remember?'

Saturday and simmered meat and vegetables didn't bear any relation to one another, at least not that she could remember, but her mother did often say odd things. She imagined the giant aluminium pot of steaming vegetables, meat, tofu, fish sausage, and boiled eggs on their kitchen table, and the bonito broth served with grated ginger, the way it was done in her mother's hometown. Homesickness clawed at her gut.

'What about you?' asked her mother.

'I'll eat soon. How's my little rascal?'

'Aya's watching *Doraemon*.'

The four-year-old was soon breathing heavily into the receiver, a stuffy nose lending her small voice a pinched, squeaky sound. Suzuki asked about the sports day, but the girl sounded pre-occupied, as if her one eye remained trained on the TV and the other on the oden pot. It was a short conversation traded in single syllables that ended with 'bye-bye'. Outgunned by oden and Doraemon, the cartoon cat with magical abilities but no ears because some nasty mice had nibbled them off, she sighed. Suzuki longed to be back in her cosy apartment.

The sunset crowd had moved on, and now only a group of youths remained, lounging against the rails, laughing and sipping from cans of cheap beer.

She resolved to cheer herself likewise.

Returning to the hotel, she bought several cans of beer from the hallway vending machine, drank one, and then dressed in her blue suit. She felt good; she felt ready. She studied the photo of the Shimizu family one final time, focusing on Yukihiro Shimizu's face. He was an attractive-looking man, of that there was no doubt, and despite his camera-shyness, she sensed a quiet strength within him. He did not look like the type of person to give up or give in easily. A man who did not want to be found would be a determined one. She pushed this thought from her mind and left the room.

Having confirmed with the desk staff the locations of her intended ports-of-call, she stepped from the hotel and into the cool Matsue night. From now, she would assume the guise of a Friday night office worker dining out on her way home.

* * *

Akabeko stood a short walk from Shinjiko Bridge. She wondered why anyone would name a sushi restaurant 'Red Cow'. At its threshold, she hesitated, acutely aware that Shimizu might be standing on the other side, running his blade across a whetting stone, watching the door, waiting. She steeled herself, parted the entrance curtains, and entered.

It was a casual place; small, with counter seating for ten diners and half-dozen tables set beneath ambient lighting. Customers in business attire sat, dining and chatting quietly. Behind the counter, two chefs, immaculate in white uniforms and boat-shaped hats, busied themselves with orders.

A sushi restaurant could be an intimidating place for solo diners; its minimalist decor, kimono-attired staff, and the seriousness of its chefs' faces demanded reverence. Reputation, Teizo had told her, was the currency through which restaurants acquired status and hired their staff. But Akabeko was not Uoshin and this caused her to wonder if Shimizu would be the type to swallow his pride and take a job beneath his station?

A demure staff in lavender kimono presented her with the menu of the day and waited politely. There was no need to fake the appearance of a hungry diner—she was ravenous. She ordered sashimi no moriawase and a chilled draught lager for starters.

Neither of the chefs, an older stern-faced man with bushy eyebrows or his young apprentice, resembled Shimizu in any shape or form. She hadn't expected to strike gold on the first swing of the pick. Instead, she sought nuggets of information. For courage, she drew out the tide on her beer glass and ordered a second. Then, in a firm voice she said, 'Excuse me, are those Shimane abalone?'

The senior chef answered. 'From Tottori Prefecture. Would you like one?'

'Perhaps later.' She smiled. 'By the way, I'm wondering if you might know of a chef by the name of Yukihiro Shimizu?' and adding quickly, 'He's an old school friend working here in Matsue.'

The older chef returned her hopeful gaze with a blank one. 'Never heard of him, sorry.' Nearby, his apprentice worked dexterously and wordlessly, laying spoonsful of glistening salmon eggs on morsels of nori-wrapped rice. The hierarchy determined who could speak and who could not.

She smiled again and thanked him politely.

Her sashimi arrived, arranged in a miniature wooden boat with the splayed wings of a flying fish as decoration. She took to it hungrily.

She had just swallowed her last morsel when another customer entered, a middle-aged man of average appearance and height, prematurely balding, and dressed in a blue suit with a lapel pin of a company whose logo she did not recognize. After he was seated at the far end of the counter, the staff took his order and in a few moments a carafe of warm sake sat before him. He poured his cup full and slurped at it noisily.

Presently, the senior chef placed a small charcoal brazier in front of him. On its grill sat a large abalone in its shell. The customer smiled and thanked him.

To Suzuki's horror, the shellfish began to squirm. The man slurped his sake, smacking his lips, watching the abalone's grey lips oscillate, expand, and contract as it twisted and turned. The brazier grew hotter, the death throes more pronounced, until the chef returned, scooped up the poor beast and ran his knife deftly through the flesh. Served as wafer-thin slices with a side saucer of soy sauce, it brought a smile to the customer's lips. He thanked the chef graciously.

Suzuki paid her bill, took her receipt, and hurriedly departed. She felt ill.

Crossing the canal, she paused to draw breath. She wished Teizo was there; not for emotional support but because his philosophical manner often helped her see things differently. 'Every town has its traditions,' he might have said, or simply, 'When in Rome….' It took a few minutes for her to clear her mind of the grotesque spectacle she'd witnessed and return to the task at hand.

Following the lamp-lit canal path, she noted the other men and women in workaday attire who passed her by. Their lonely faces and solemn strides perhaps marked them as *tenkin* employees, those unfortunates whose companies posted them to far-flung offices throughout the archipelago, away from their families and friends, to sacrifice a year or more of their lives in order to advance themselves in the company. Tenkin postings could be a grim prospect, but there was an upside. To be a stranger in a strange town was to be free of the demands and obligations that home and community piled on a person; it was the place for privacy and to have time to oneself. Life was a highway where one could join the rank-and-file in their mad rush to a meaningless existence and sacrifice for family and company—or one could simply turn off and tune out.

After three more restaurants, her enthusiasm for seafood began to wane. No leads had been forthcoming, and the only thing that hadn't diminished was the size of her stomach. Although she had paced herself wisely by ordering light dishes, after her fourth restaurant she began to suspect that Shimizu hadn't chosen to 'evaporate' in Matsue at all. None of the chefs she'd spoken to had ever heard of a newcomer to their local culinary scene, let alone one by the name of Yukihiro Shimizu.

Sushi Mondo would be her final stop.

It was a big and bustling place, far less intimate than the previous ones. It was also not strictly a sushiya, but rather a seafood smorgasbord whereby diners chose the ingredients and had them prepared to their whims and fancies. Suzuki requested for a counter seat, giving her a front-row view of the ice beds where whole fish, prawns, crab, and scallops lay fresh and glistening.

She ordered deep-fried scampi with a yuzu dipping sauce, a small basket of vegetable tempura with bamboo salt, and a half bottle of Izumo dry sake to help them on their way.

Not one of the small army of chefs remotely resembled Shimizu. Fending off thoughts that her intuition might have failed her, she forced herself on the tender titbits of crispy squid.

Her phone vibrated.

She glanced at the screen—'caller unknown'. Swallowing quickly, she said, 'Yes?'

'Ms Suzuki?'

'Yes?'

'It's Sota Shimizu. Sorry to call you at this late hour. I have something. It might be nothing but....'

'What is it?'

'I found some photos of Dad. They're of his student days—parties and picnics with friends.'

'Go on.'

'Four of the photos seemed to have been taken at the same location, probably years apart.'

'Matsue?'

'It looks like the Izumo Taisha Shrine. It's hard to tell. They don't show the whole shrine, just Dad holding a fishing rod in front of it.'

'Can you send me the most recent?'

'I'll do it right away.'

She thanked him again, promised to call his mother on Sunday evening with an update, and said goodbye.

The image arrived soon after. It was an old Fujifilm snapshot, faded and glared by the light under which Sota had photographed it. His father stood suntanned and smiling, rod in hand, beneath the gigantic straw shimenawa rope of the Shinto shrine's entranceway. There were two others, classmates perhaps, standing on either side of him holding their own tackle, all smiling broadly at the camera.

Suzuki laid down her chopsticks. To the chef in front of her, a young man with an angular jaw and quick eyes, she said, 'This is wonderful tempura. Are these vegetables grown locally?' It was the kind of question any tourist or a company employee on tenkin posting might ask.

'They certainly are,' he replied.

'I was just wondering ... you wouldn't happen to know where this photo was taken?' She held up her phone.

He leant forward and his eyes narrowed. 'Looks like Izumo Taisha to me.' Then said, 'No, my mistake. That's Miho Taisha Shrine.'

'Is it near here?'

'It's in Mihonoseki, about an hour's drive up the coast. Are you planning a visit?'

'Is it worth it?'

'The village is pretty. It's a popular place for hobby fishermen.'

'Anything special about the shrine?'

He grinned. 'It's a *power spot*. People believe it's a source of spiritual energy that brings good luck and health to those who pray there.'

'You believe that?'

He laughed out loud. 'Let's just say, in my profession I'll pray for anything that brings fishermen good luck.'

She thanked him, apologizing for keeping him from his work. But before moving off, he added, 'There's a nice lighthouse cafe on the cape. On a clear day you can see all the way to the Oki Islands. I recommend it.'

As she chewed her last piece of squid, a quick online search confirmed his remarks.

Miho Taisha Shrine is the head shrine of more than three thousand Ebisu shrines nationwide and enshrines the god of maritime safety, large fishing catches, and business prosperity.

She recalled the tiny shrine on Teizo's uncle's shop wall. The Shinto connection hummed like a live wire in her head. It was time to venture further afield. She glanced at her watch: 9 p.m. She lifted her phone, pressed 'call history' and tapped the number.

'Sota? It's Mami Suzuki. Thanks for the photo. It's helpful. Listen—did your father ever mention a shrine named Miho Taisha in Mihonoseki?'

There was a pause and the young man said, 'No ... but he might have to Mum. She's out with a friend. I'll ask her when she gets back.'

She thanked him again, wished him a good night, and ended the call. She finished her sake and called for the bill. She wondered who Rumi Shimizu might be seeing at this hour on a Friday night.

* * *

The night air had acquired a chilly freshness and Suzuki hoped it would aid her digestion. The tide had lifted the level of the canal so that its soft gurgle followed her as she kept to the stone lamps lining the path back to Shinjiko Bridge.

Ahead of her, a figure approached. It weaved in and out of the weeping willow trees, seemingly aimless in direction, until revealing itself in the lamplight. It halted, wavering.

'Excuse me.' The man's voice was as uneven as his walk.

She slowed but did not stop. 'Yes?'

'You dined at Akabeko tonight.'

'That's right....' She glimpsed at his drooping lips, discerning the slurred sounds that passed through them.

'The food was marvellous, wasn't it?'

She nodded but kept moving.

'Would you happen to be free for a drink?'

'No—I'm on my way home.' She quickened her pace. 'Creep,' she muttered.

Shinjiko Bridge loomed ahead, garishly lit and devoid of foot traffic. She hurried towards it, not slowing until she was halfway across. Glancing back, she gasped. The creep had climbed the steps. He waved hopefully from the end of the bridge and took an unsteady step towards her.

Her chest tightened.

She broke into a run, wishing she had worn her Asics 'gumshoes', and did not stop until she reached the end of the bridge. She descended the stairway into a pedestrian underpass and scurried through its mouse-hole entrance, the hollow echo of her heels chasing her frantic shadow through to the esplanade on the other side.

Never had she been gladder to smell the fake florals of hotel carpet deodorizer. The night duty staff of the Sunrise Hotel, bemused at the sight of a breathless businesswoman leaping into the lift, bid her a 'welcome back' and 'good night' in a single breath.

On reaching her floor, she hurried into her room and secured the door latch.

Was she overreacting? Not in a strange city. Not with a drunk male in pursuit. They were the bane of a working woman's life. Sooner or later, one would cross their kind in a Sannomiya bar or izakaya. The leering came first, then the compliments of youthful beauty, and with more imbibing, questions of 'husbands' and 'boyfriends', and finally the insidious probing of one's views on uwaki—secret affairs and one-night stands. One was supposed to laugh them off. To show anger was to let them win, in which event they would grin sympathetically and call themselves an impolite fool, or baka, and apologize. Not even corporate-sponsored parties were safe, and she pitied the female staff who had to mop up the vomit of a drunken senior colleague, then have to apologize on their behalf to the restaurant or bar staff. She vowed to never put herself in such a position, especially where a male colleague, or God forbid, a stranger, could use inebriation as an excuse to lay a hand on her body.

After bathing and dressing in her pyjamas, she felt better. She sat down at the window desk and opened a can of beer. Lake Shinji's shoreline sparkled like gemstones on black velvet in the distance, the esplanade lights trailing away in a wide arc before merging into the outer suburbs of the city. An occasional car motored across Shinjiko Bridge, but neither a pedestrian nor its shadow moved. She admonished herself for not having called a taxi from the last restaurant.

She opened her laptop and ran a quick search for 'Mihonoseki'. The Sushi Mondo chef's words reappeared: it was a small fishing community clustered around a crescent-shaped cove and located thirty-two kilometres from Matsue. Miho Taisha's scale surprised her. The shrine's shimenawa was immense, resembling a fat, twisted worm, and the vast thatched roof of its *haiden*, the worshipping hall, seemed almost to float among the canopy of the surrounding trees.

Next, she turned to logistics. Naturally, a rental car would be easiest. Mindful of costs, however, she turned to the city bus schedule instead. Solving cases was as much about meditating on facts as it was unearthing them; a seaside bus journey would do nicely.

A knock sounded at the door.

She caught her startled face in the window reflection. She shot a glance at the bed clock—10.16 p.m. Padding silently to the door, she peered through the fisheye spyhole. The hallway was empty. She stepped back, her pulse leaping. A second rap of knuckles made her almost cry out. She drew back to the spyhole. A young man in a hotel uniform stood holding a tray in his hands.

'Yes?' she said, unevenly.

'Mr Matsumoto?'

'Pardon me?'

'Mr Takahiko Matsumoto?'

She opened the door to the extent of the security latch.

'No—it's Suzuki.'

He glanced nervously at the paper docket on his tray. Her gaze fell to the trainee badge on his lapel. She unlocked the door, reached out, and turned the slip of paper upside down.

'Try 9-0-9,' she said. 'You'll find a hungry Mr Matsumoto there.'

He apologized, thanking her profusely, and retreated to the lift, leaving the aroma of Matsumoto's chicken cutlet on rice to linger.

She returned to the window table and for the second time that night felt the draining effect of nervous exhaustion. There was now the matter of accommodation to sort out. Mihonoseki had several small inns, and she selected the cheapest, the prehistoric-looking Mihokan. Within moments she had secured lodging for one night, pleased with herself for claiming the fifteen per cent online discount. She closed her laptop and turned to the lake. To believe that Shimizu had returned to the place of his youth was a long shot. No, it was more than a long shot; it was like wishing for a bullseye with a blindfold on.

Nostalgia rarely 'evaporated'. Fond memories of visiting Mihonoseki, she reasoned, might just have motivated Shimizu to seek comfort in the familiar. She drained the dregs of her beer, permitted herself a small belch, then brushed her teeth and slipped between the cool, starched sheets. For some odd reason, she recalled a Hindu proverb Teizo had once quoted: 'Exhaustion makes the best pillow.' But any wisdom she hoped to gain from it faded with her consciousness.

* * *

She rose at dawn, breakfasting at the hotel's Skylounge buffet with a handful of like-minded early birds, perched at the window counter.

Across the blue-grey surface of the lake, tiny craft boats drifted in dozens, each poled by a single boatman. They appeared to be fishing for something. Beyond the lake, the land rose into a soft mist, so that the mountains of the Chūgoku Sanchi seemed to float on every shade of blue imaginable. It was a sight one would expect in the Land of the Gods.

It was not until she crossed Shinjiko Bridge did she realize that the boatmen weren't poling, but probing. Stepping to the rail, she watched one hoist his netted scoop and pour a multitude of tiny clams into a plastic tub. The fizzing sound they made reminded her of Teizo's uncle mentioning Matsue's famed shijimi clams. Suzuki guessed that she'd probably eaten them in her miso soup that morning.

At a little after 8 a.m., she bought a convenience-store coffee and boarded the bus for Mihonoseki outside Matsue train station. Save for two teenage boys with backpacks and fishing rods, the passengers were mostly elderly and quiet. At the back of the bus, she spread out her tourist map and began to study it.

But as the driver pulled away from the station, he braked suddenly. Passengers gasped.

'Shit!' She spilled her coffee.

Hurrying towards them, waving, was a man in a blue suit with a suitcase. He climbed aboard the bus, excusing himself, and shunted his scuffed valise down the aisle to a few seats in front of her.

At the sight of her stalker from the night before, her gaze hardened. Her breath quickened and a momentary paralysis overcame her. She hurriedly slipped on a pair of tortoiseshell sunglasses and a face mask.

As the bus passed down the leafy avenues of preserved
samurai residences, period museums, and shophouses, her fear
turned to anger. By the time they skirted Nakaumi, the wide
inlet in which Lake Shinji's waters mixed with the Sea of Japan,
she was ready to berate this creep seated in front of her; to tell
him—and the entire bus—why chasing women down darkened
streets was not some sadistic entertainment, like watching a
shellfish be cooked to death.

It was illegal.

She drew a deep breath and calmed herself. A public display
of outrage would only bring unwanted attention. Good private
investigators were like assassins—timing and discipline were
paramount. So, too, was a working knowledge of the land.
Granted, a fishing village at the tip of a narrow peninsular might
have been a one-ticket for an assassin in olden times, but this
bothered her less than the man in front of her, whose balding
head bobbed like a greasy fishing buoy. Privately, she wished she
was *his* assassin.

The bus hugged the coastline, passing in and out of
fishing hamlets and small coves where colourful dinghies lay
beached on the shore. Then the road straightened, and a traffic
bridge appeared. It was a long bridge that reached across a
narrow strait to Sakaiminato, the westernmost port of Tottori
Prefecture. Against its long wharf a trawler fleet rested, as
forklifts and small trucks moved in choreographed madness
in and out the warehouses. This confirmed what she'd read
the previous night—that Sakaiminato was the hub of a serious
seafood trade.

A while later, they pulled into a village community centre
and the city service terminated. To Suzuki's dismay, only four
passengers transferred to the waiting community bus for
Mihonoseki: the teenage fishers, the creep in the blue suit—and

herself. She took advantage of their restroom visit to board the bus and claim the rear seat. Face mask and sunglasses firmly affixed, she buried her head in her map.

The peninsular narrowed. Soon, the road was no more than a grey ribbon following the contours of the coastline, forcing itself between boulders and passing within metres of the foaming shore break.

The passengers dozed, but Suzuki felt her senses prickling. She had until Sunday afternoon to prove her hunch correct. Whatever the outcome, she'd have to be back aboard the 'Swinging Yakumo' by Sunday afternoon in order to reach Kobe by evening.

Her thoughts were thrown into sudden darkness as the bus entered a tunnel. She gasped as it burst out the other side and into a vision of a timeless Japan. Ahead lay a tiled-roof village hemmed between lush hills and the sea, sheltered within a crescent harbour where fishing boats, yachts, and dinghies of all colours and sizes drifted at mooring lines. Shops and hotels—quaint buildings from the age of the rickshaw and palanquin—lined its shore. It was here, outside the imposing Meishinkan 'Morning God Hotel', that the driver brought the small bus to a halt.

Suzuki lingered, allowing the others to disembark and disperse before her. The teenagers disappeared into a laneway guesthouse; and the creep in the blue suit into the foyer of the Meishinkan.

Thanking the Seven Gods of Good Luck, she wheeled her suitcase away towards the Mihokan, a grand old structure that stood on the high tide mark at the far end of the esplanade. For a hundred-year-old inn, it was both elegant and homely, and it caused her to wonder how such a charming relic was not listed on Japan's largest online hotel booking site.

The female staff at the reception desk greeted her warmly, and after confirming her reservation, led her up a creaking stairway to a large tatami mat room with an indoor veranda and a harbour view. It was perfect.

The woman returned moments later and set down a small teapot, cup and a sweet bean cake on the veranda table.

Thanking her, Suzuki then asked, 'Is Miho Taisha far?'

'A minute's walk. Just follow Aoishidatami-dori Street behind the hotel. It will take you directly there.'

'What time does it close?'

'Oh, it never closes.'

As the woman turned to leave, Suzuki caught her. 'I was just wondering….'

'Yes?'

'You wouldn't happen to know of a man by the name of Yukihiro Shimizu, by any chance?'

The woman's eyelids flickered. It was a near imperceptible movement, almost insect-like. 'Is he a fisherman?' she asked softly. 'We get many from Sakaiminato stopping over.'

'He's an old school friend. We attended Shimane University together.'

The woman shook her head. 'Not that I know of.' She smiled warmly. 'Enjoy your stay at the Mihokan. Dinner will be served in your room at 6.30 p.m.'

Suzuki listened to the woman's footsteps descend the stairs. She sat down to her tea and cake, contemplating what she'd just witnessed.

* * *

Now, a little before noon, the autumn sun bathed the room in warm, earthy tones. A hanging scroll in the alcove depicted the passage of a piece junk between pine-clad outcrops, a timeless scene that left little to the imagination if one were to look outside. She slid back the window, allowing the cool sea air to venture in.

Across the water came the sound of hammer on steel, a propeller thrummed, and a lone seagull cried beyond the sea wall. There was sudden laughter beneath her window. She peered down to find two fisherwomen busy hanging glistening white squid on drying lines.

But the small pleasures of village life were not hers to savour, and soon she was pacing the blue flagstones of Aoishidatami-dori Street, which passed through the neighbourhood behind the inn. Shops and houses cast the path in shade, but where sunlight pooled, fisherwomen laid horse mackerel soaked in sake on wire mesh grills to dry and shooed away cats.

Suzuki passed beneath an archway and moved towards a broad pathway lined with camphor trees, which led towards the Miho Taisha Shrine. Beneath a towering Shinto gateway, she offered a short bow. She considered herself no more spiritual than the next Japanese—which wasn't a lot, because, despite Shinto rituals and traditions being part of life's celebrations, few gave much thought to the eight million deities said to inhabit the natural world. City life, afterall, was a godless life.

At the top of the path, she climbed the stone steps and passed beneath the enormous, twisted shimenawa rope. No breeze followed her through the doorway and into a wide pebbled courtyard.

Miho Taisha was unlike any bustling big city Shinto shrine. Weathered and salt-stained and topped by a sloping roof of moss-covered wood tiles, its vast worshipping hall—the haiden—resembled something ancient and living, inside of which one might commune with the gods.

Yet, there were few worshippers here. Save for the flitter of white-eyed *mejiro* at the forest's edge, all was quiet and still.

Suzuki found the eeriness strangely comforting; like strolling through a cemetery—alone, but not alone.

She climbed the steps of the haiden and at the altar tossed a fifty-yen coin into the offerings box. Waggling the rope, she set the bell clanging, clapped twice and bowed. She could discern no visible difference between the scene in front of her and the image that Sota Shimizu had sent her. Miho Taisha stood exactly as it had thirty-five years ago.

A sudden commotion arrested her thoughts. She turned to find the teenage fishers outside the shrine office on the far side of the courtyard. Their backpacks were gone, and they carried only their fishing rods and tackle boxes in hand. Suzuki wandered over.

'Off fishing?' she asked.

Perhaps not recognizing her without her face mask and sunglasses, they replied stiffly, 'Yes.' They had been hovering over a display of omamori amulets and small wooden ema plaques. Now each boy held in his hand a blue silk amulet embroidered with a leaping red snapper.

'Praying for a big fish?'

'Sure am.'

She wished them luck, and once they'd made their purchases and moved on, she picked out an amulet and said to the young priest behind the counter, 'I'll take this one, please.'

A short while later, having penned messages on their ema and hung them with dozens of others on a rack, the two fishers approached her. 'Sorry to ask, but would you take our photo?' one asked, holding out his phone.

'Sure,' she smiled.

As she framed the scene, it occurred to her that it was almost identical to the Shimizu image: two teenagers side-by-side, rods and tackle boxes in hands, sunlight illuminating their happy, hopeful faces.

She waited until they had gone before reading their messages to the gods.

Today I hope to catch my personal best—a huge snapper! and *a big fish for dinner, please!*

There were others, too.

Thank you for honouring my wish. I caught many fish today and *a huge suzuki—thank you!*

The thought of sharing her surname with a species of sea bass made Suzuki smile wryly. The kanji characters for 'Suzu' and 'ki' differed from her own, but her first name, 'Ma', meaning true, and 'mi', beauty, made her feel sufficiently armed. She hoped Ebisu might smile on her endeavours.

A single restaurant served the village of Mihonoseki. This was because tourists and sightseers were inclined to pay for dinner and breakfast at their hotel or guesthouse. The small shop stood at a junction of three pathways at the end of Aoishidatami-dori Street. It was cosy and clean, with tables and a window counter that looked down the laneway to the harbour.

The staff took Suzuki's order of a basket of tempura seafood and enquired cheerfully, 'Here on holiday?' She wore a colourful apron and headscarf, and her jolly face was all flushed and tan.

'Yes, I am,' Suzuki replied.

'Have you been to the lighthouse?'

'Is it nice?'

'Everyone goes. There's a wonderful cafe, too.'

'So I've been hearing....'

A phone rang and the woman excused herself, leaving Suzuki to overhear her take orders for a party of fishermen who would soon be arriving. She finished her meal, paid, and collected her receipt but at the threshold, she paused. 'Excuse me for asking, but I'm looking for an old friend. His name is Yukihiro Shimizu. Would you happen to know him?'

The woman glanced up quickly, and for a moment her face was unreadable.

'He's a Shimane University old boy—like me,' Suzuki said.

'Is that so?' The woman pursed her lips and shook her head. 'I'm afraid I've never met anyone by that name.'

Suzuki left feeling pensive, the morning's events and idiosyncrasies occupying her thoughts all the way to the harbour. There, a charter boat had drawn alongside the sea wall and its half-dozen fishermen were now disembarking. Beyond their laughing and shouting, was a father crouched with his young daughter at the water edge, staring down at the tinsel-coloured fish which flashed back and forth between the barnacled mooring posts. The girl's cries of 'Sakana! Sakana!' filled Suzuki with a sudden longing to be home.

She continued to the end of the esplanade and climbed the steps to the breakwater. At intervals, anglers stood with their tackle boxes and canvas buckets, meditating on the gentle swell, and to each she nodded a greeting. No matter that they stood solemn and to themselves, the fishermen returned the greeting to the female tourist in the salmon-pink hat and tortoiseshell sunglasses. They were tall and reedy, short and heavy, dark-haired, dyed-haired, balding—but not one resembled a master sushi chef. Not one of them looked out of place standing with a rod in their hand before the easy swells of the Sea of Japan.

Reaching the stone lantern at the end of the breakwater, she found the two teenagers.

'Any luck?' she asked.

They looked up and grinned, and one of them nodded towards a small collapsible bucket. 'Two snapper and a sea bass.'

'Great! What'll you do with them?'

'The guesthouse chef said he'd prepare them for our dinner.'

Suzuki peered down at the three fish, fat and boggle-eyed, oblivious to their fate that lay in the sure hands of the chef and the cold edge of his knife. She glanced back at the village. What better place for a runaway sushi chef to hide than in a sleepy fishing village with a sideline in spiritual tourism and hobby-fishing.

But something bothered her about this possibility. Shimizu had committed no crime, so why would he come all the way here and assume a new identity? Mihonoseki wasn't downtown Osaka; it was familiar territory and the locals would know him.

And yet none did.

She glanced at her watch. Dinner would be served in a short while. Until then she would make some phone calls and rest up for the evening's adventure.

Back in her room she poured a cup of roasted green tea and stepped onto the veranda. The dial tone had hardly run before he answered.

'Manning the radio room 24/7 now, are we?' she said.

'I'm waiting for an SOS,' he replied.

His voice cheered her up.

'You'll have to wait a bit longer. I have a question for you.'

'Former lieutenant-commander Teizo Yasuhara of the Japanese Maritime Self Defence Force, at your service.'

'Okay. Listen—I know we return amulets to the shrine when their luck expires, but does it matter *where* we return them?'

'An omamori should be returned to the god from whose shrine it was acquired. Are you at Izumo Taisha?'

'I'm in Mihonoseki—can't talk now. Got another call to make—' She caught herself. 'Thanks for the information. You're always helpful.'

No sooner had she said goodbye than she stole a sip of her tea and pressed 'Rumi Shimizu'. Her mind ticked with the dial tone. The pick-up was quick, the voice taut. 'Is everything alright?' it said.

'All is well. Do you have time to speak?'

'Yes, yes, of course.'

'Does the village of Mihonoseki mean anything to you?'

'I've heard of it. I don't recall where. You're still in Shimane?'

'Yes. Would you say that your husband is a spiritual man?'

'Not more than the average person. Why?'

'I mean, does he make a habit of praying at shrines?'

'I doubt he would go out of his way to pray at one.'

'Does he keep any omamori?'

Silence followed, then, 'Yes, he does … he keeps one on his side table, hanging from the bed light.'

'Can you describe it?'

'It's blue with a red fish on it.'

'Is it still there?'

'Just a moment … I'll check.'

Suzuki listened to the sound of footsteps, a door sliding open, items being shuffled, then Rumi Shimizu's breathless voice: 'It's gone.'

A creaking of floorboards sounded on the landing outside Suzuki's room and a voice called softly from behind the sliding door. She apologized to Rumi Shimizu, thanked her and ended the call.

'Yes?' she said.

'Dinner is served.' The voice materialized into the woman from the reception, attired in a patterned blue apron and headscarf. From a trolley in the entranceway, she delivered trays of small dishes, which she arranged on the low table at the centre of the room. It was the quintessential fishing village feast, a sprawling array of seafood prepared every which way and presented with perfection.

Suzuki's request for a small bottle of sake was met with a knowing smile, and in a short while, she was sipping chilled rice wine brewed by the Shingon Buddhist monks of distant Mount Daisen.

She ate slowly, her senses attuned to the subtle flavours of the sauces and dressings that elevated each ingredient to heavenly excellence: tuna sashimi of the most intense ruby red served with a smoky soy sauce, octopus as tender as wagyu beef accompanied by fresh ground wasabi root, and sea urchin eggs, whose creaminess defied description.

Pausing to rest her stomach, she poured more sake and took out her phone. She pondered, once more, about the photo that Sota Shimizu had sent her of his father and the two fellow fishers. Three happy youths....

Lifting the glass to her lips, she held it suspended. The boy on Yukihiro Shimizu's right-hand side looked oddly familiar. Her eyes widened. She leapt up from the table, spilling her sake, gathered her jacket and hurried from the room.

* * *

Glowing paper lanterns now lined the blue flagstones of Aoishidatami-dori Street. She scurried past them, taking the stone steps to the shrine two at a time, until she entered the pebbled courtyard. A soft light emanated from the office window where the silhouette of a priest sat reading. He glanced up at the sound of her footsteps.

'Good evening,' he said.

'Good evening,' she said breathlessly. 'I visited earlier….'

'I recognize you.'

She lifted a blue amulet tied with white cord and embroidered with the red fish emblem. 'One more of these, please.' The priest regarded her curiously, took her money and passed her the small paper packet containing the charm.

It was a feeble attempt at disguising her intentions, but time was against her. She held up her phone. 'This photo was taken here. I was wondering if you might know the people in it?'

He leant forwards, peering at her glowing screen. 'It was taken before my time, I'm afraid.' He looked back at her. 'Just one moment.' He slid open the door behind him and called to someone.

Presently, an elderly man appeared.

'This is the *kannushi*,' said the priest.

She bowed in reverence to the head priest, and after their exchange of greetings, the young priest repeated her question to him. She enlarged the image of the boys' faces, holding it out for him to see.

The old man's face was thoughtful. 'I don't know who the others are, but this person I do know. As a matter of fact, she lives here in Mihonoseki.'

'She?'

The priest's finger hovered over the youth on Shimizu's right-hand side—the boy with the sparkling eyes, slim neck, and short hair—the one that had caused her to flinch over dinner.

'Why, this is Yumiko Matsudaira,' he said.

'Where can I find her?'

'Where are you staying?'

'The Mihokan.'

'Then it shouldn't be too hard—she's the owner.'

* * *

It was a little after 8 p.m. The sky was clear and star-filled, and there were no worshippers about. Crickets chirped in symphony from the forest's edge. All was still.

With adrenalin goading her to return to the Mihokan as quickly as possible, she made for the entranceway. But a strange and sudden compulsion caused her to hesitate at the threshold. She turned around and walked back across the courtyard to the haiden. She fumbled and took out a coin from her purse, tossed it into the offerings box, set the bell clanging, clapped and bowed. Suzuki wished for the improbable—not the impossible.

Then an odd thing happened: a breeze grazed her cheek. She glanced up to see the white paper *shide* streamers rustle overhead. She felt the hairs on her nape twinge and she shivered. *Kaminazuki*, the Month of the Gods. Beyond the altar, the inner sanctum of the haiden loomed like the gullet of a great fish, its ribcage of ancient cypress beams stretching far back into the darkness. It was from these fragrant depths that the breeze seemed to emanate.

She bowed, deeper than before, and quickly departed.

The lanterns lining the pathway had been extinguished, leaving only the weak glow of tungsten light bulbs to illuminate the way back to the Mihokan. But on arrival, she found the old inn in darkness. The foyer was empty, the reception desk shuttered, and only the foot lamps beside the wall had been left on. She stepped back into the street and looked up, searching for a lighted window, but there were none.

A bell jingled.

Laughter and loud voices sounded at the end of Aoishidatami-dori Street. She made her way towards them and in a few moments arrived outside 'Fukuda Liquor, Sake, Soy Sauce, Vinegar'. Peering in, she saw that it was less a shop than a grotto. Shelves of bottles, jars, and flagons climbed its iodine-coloured walls, and within their smoke-filled confines, a huddle of fishers stood drinking. At the back of the store, a high counter separated an elderly man, the owner perhaps, from a large customer in a mint-green uniform.

Suzuki made a snap decision.

She slid back the door and set the bell jingling. The fishers returned her 'good evening' with courteous nods, but quickly resumed their conversations.

She stepped to a shelf and lifted a bottle of soy sauce, faking interest in its label.

'Locally brewed,' said the bartender.

'Is that so?' Suzuki replied. She carried it to the counter. 'I'll take this, and a large bottle of Kirin lager—to have here, please.'

The big man in the mint-green uniform nodded his approval but said nothing. He raised his glass and drained it.

'Visiting?' enquired the barman, placing a frosted bottle and glass on the counter in front of her.

'Yes.'

He levered off the cap. 'Come far?'

'From Matsue.'

'Everyone's from Matsue today.'

'Oh?'

A toilet flushed at the rear of the shop and a small door opened. To Suzuki's horror, the creep in the blue suit emerged. Without washing his hands, he stepped to the counter and resumed drinking beside the big man. He seemed not to have noticed her, and for all the tea south of Tokyo, she wished that he wouldn't!

But it was too late.

He placed his glass down on the counter, gave a satisfied sigh and licked his lips. Glancing in her direction, his eyebrows lifted. 'From Matsue?'

She poured her glass full and emptied it in three swallows. The barman and the big man exchanged glances.

'Yes,' she said, wiping the foam from her lip.

'By bus?' asked the bartender.

She nodded, refilling her glass.

'Funny, I didn't see you,' said the creep. 'There's only one bus a day and I was on it.'

'Maybe you were hungover,' she replied.

The barman and big man guffawed.

'Touché, Madame.' The creep's lips glistened.

The beer had fortified her. 'So, what brings you here?' she asked.

'Business.'

'He sells ice-making machines to our fishing cooperative,' the big man added.

'Is that so?' said Suzuki.

'Do you need an industrial ice-maker?' the creep asked her.

'Doesn't every modern woman?'

'I have brochures in my hotel room....'

'Your card will be fine.'

He could hardly conceal his glee. Moving closer, close enough for her to smell the sourness on his body, he purred, 'Junichiro Maeda, Sales, Fuji Systems'. He presented her with his card. 'And you—what's your purpose here?'

'I'm visiting the Miho Taisha Shrine.'

'It's most beautiful under starlight.' His forehead shone beneath the strip light. 'Would you care to visit later?'

She turned to the bartender. 'I'm also looking out for an old school friend. Perhaps you might know him? A Yukihiro Shimizu?'

The bartender shot a glance at the big man; they both shook their heads.

'Well then,' the creep interrupted, 'let's drink to old friends and new.' His gaze roamed the contours of her body. 'Another round, mister bartender—on me!'

She drained her glass, slipped his business card into her pocket, reminding herself to wash hands later, and said, 'Sorry. Early to bed, early to rise.' She paid, collected her bottle of soy sauce and departed through the fog of tobacco smoke.

The chilly sea air was an elixir. She set off briskly along the darkened path, keen to put as much distance as she could between herself and the despicable man in the crumpled blue suit. But the alley divided into two paths, forcing her to stop and reconsider. She recognized neither. It was then she heard a doorbell jingle and the door slam shut. Footsteps sounded.

'Shit!'

She broke into a run, her pulse leaping ahead of her. She took the decline, reasoning that the path would bring her to the sea. The alleyway lurched left and right, growing ever narrower as it pushed between fishing shacks. Cold panic now gripped her. She stumbled. The night sky's brilliance, snuffed out by the leaning houses, meant she could see nothing. Their overhanging eaves crowded in on her and not a lamp glowed inside any of them.

She reached a T-intersection.

Left, or right?

The footsteps drummed louder behind her, tempo quickening. Repressing a whimper, she chose right. But a hand caught her by the arm. A scream rose in her throat. She pivoted, fists balled, ready to fight, but the face in the slither of starlight was not of a man—it belonged to the woman from the Mihokan.

'Forgive me,' she said breathlessly. 'I followed you from the hotel.' Her grip on Suzuki's arm softened and gently guided it back towards the left path. 'My name is Yumiko Matsudaira. I understand you would like to speak with me?'

Suzuki could not bring herself to speak—not yet. She allowed the woman to guide her through the labyrinth until the path reconnected with the flagstones of Aoishidatami-dori Street. On entering the Mihokan, Matsudaira said quietly, 'It is best that we go to your room.'

Once inside, Suzuki saw that her dinner dishes had been cleared away, the table moved aside, and a futon laid out on the tatami floor and turned down. The paper doors to the veranda had been drawn closed.

The two women now stood facing each other but it was Matsudaira who spoke first.

'May I ask your reason for being here in Mihonoseki?' Her tone neither hostile nor fearful, but merely that of one woman asking to another a simple question.

'I'm a private investigator from Kobe. My client's husband has disappeared, and I've been tasked with finding him. That's all.'

'And what will you do when you find him?'

'Notify his wife and family. I don't wish to make contact with him.'

A cane chair creaked on the other side of the paper doors. Suzuki flinched.

'You already have, Ms Suzuki,' said a voice on the veranda.

A lamp turned on. The doors parted. Before her stood a huge man in a traditional indigo *samue* vest and pants. His close-cropped hair brushed the lintel.

'You have met my half-sister. Now here I am,' revealed Yukihiro Shimizu.

Suzuki glanced at Matsudaira whose face was now grave.

Shimizu stepped into the light. 'You do realize that a formal complaint to the police is all it will take to have your private investigator's registration cancelled,' he threatened. 'Disturbing the peace. Isn't that what they call stalking?'

'You're in *my* room,' Suzuki said.

He smiled wryly. To Matsudaira, he said in a gentle tone, 'O-nechan, thank you. You did the right thing. Now, could I kindly request a bottle of sake and two glasses, please?'

The woman gave a quick nod and departed.

'I apologize for intruding on you, but under the circumstances it was the best way,' Shimizu said. He motioned to the two chairs on the veranda. 'Let's sit a while, shall we?'

They faced each other over the small table, and through the opened window came the sound of a soughing tide. The harbour gleamed like quicksilver under the starlight.

'Don't you think it's a little amateur to walk around a small village asking for me by name?' he said.

'It's contrarian.'

'How so?'

'You can't force a clam to open, you have to make it open by itself.' She had calmed herself and was now watching him. 'It's harder to hide in a small village than in a big city, even if the locals are on your side. In the end, I could only surmise that you wanted to be found. Since gossip travels faster than I ever could, I put out the word by asking around.'

'But how did you know I was here—in Mihonoseki?'

'Your omamori was missing.'

Surprise flashed across his face. 'Well, it's customary to return one when its luck expires.'

'Is that why you left your family?'

He reached inside his vest and pulled out a pack of Camel Lights and a lighter. 'May I smoke?'

'Normally I'd say no, but under the circumstances….'

He apologized and drew the window open wider, allowing the cool night air to eddy across the veranda. He placed a cigarette between his lips, lit it, and drew deeply. As he blew the smoke through the window, a pained look filled his face.

'You'll appreciate that it's a little more complicated than that. But let's be clear on one thing, I'm not running from anything. I came running *to something*. I came to make amends, to heal an old wound between kin before it was too late. Ms Matsudaira … Yumiko and I share the same mother; we are blood. Years ago, we had a falling out that never repaired itself—I blame myself for that—and because of it she was afraid to make contact with me.'

'Your wife didn't mention this.'

'She doesn't know.' He drew on the cigarette and exhaled with a sigh. 'It's a long story—too long even for an autumn night. Suffice to say, when Yumiko told me someone had arrived looking for me, she was worried. She advised me to hurry back to Matsue. I told her, no. It was time.'

'Time for what?'

The door slid open, and Matsudaira entered bearing a tray with a bottle of chilled sake and two glasses. After she had set them on the table, he thanked her warmly. Sensing all was well, she excused herself and closed the door quietly behind her.

The sake bottle looked like a toy in Shimizu's grasp. His large frame set the chair creaking with every movement. He poured her glass, then his own.

'You didn't finish answering the question,' she said.

'I didn't start.' He raised his glass. 'To the vagaries of life.'

She reciprocated.

He took a sip and placed his cup down gently.

'In the culinary world there is a traditional technique for killing live fish. We call it *shinkei-jime*—the art of severing the central nerve in order to paralyse the fish, thus preserving its freshness and umami flavour. Paralysis is what I have endured. Life performed its own shinkei-jime on me. I was flesh, blood, and bone but with no feeling. I was unable to move forwards, backwards, or decide anything for myself. I felt only an obligation to keep working, providing, enduring—until I could endure no longer. Then I had an epiphany. I realized that I had the power to drop everything and walk away. I didn't need to kill myself.'

'And now here you are.'

'Yes, and I'm alive! This isn't about self-pity. This is about self-preservation. I could have killed myself or died a slow agonizing death from overwork and hard drinking, like the other chefs I know. So, I asked myself: what am I worth if I am dead? Nothing! That is why I came here. I decided to make amends, to start anew. Now, I help my half-sister in the evenings and work at the cafe on the cape during the day.

'The Lighthouse Cafe?'

'On a clear day, you can see all the way to Oki Islands.'

'So I've heard. It was you who prepared my dinner tonight wasn't it?'

He lifted his cup and drained it. He offered her a second, but she declined.

'Will you make contact?' she asked.

'With my family? Yes. But I would like you to do it first.'

'Why?'

'I'm paying you, aren't I?'

'Your wife earns a salary....'

'Ha! I doubt it would be spent on trying to find me,' he snorted. 'You're married?'

'Not anymore.'

'Then you'll know that life doesn't always go to plan. If Rumi wants a divorce, she can have it.'

She frowned. 'Why would she want a divorce?'

'She didn't tell you?' His gaze shifted back to the harbour, and he nodded to himself. 'No, I'm sure she wouldn't have.'

Suzuki waited.

'She has been having an affair for more than a year now.'

'Are you certain?'

'I have even seen them together in Osaka.'

'Someone you know?'

'An associate of hers. A younger guy. Works in the pearl business.'

Her eyebrows leapt skyward. The idea too outrageous! Danno?

Shimizu laughed. 'What's wrong? You needn't worry about me. I apologize if all this raises bad feelings. It is as much my fault.'

'Meaning?'

'All I do is work, eat, sleep, work. I'd never have had time for an affair even if I'd wanted one. Between Rumi and I, there is no love anymore. It burnt out years ago. Now that the kids are older, they'll understand. They're ready to face life on their own terms.'

'You miss them, don't you?'

'My children? Have you met them?'

She nodded.

'Do they miss me?'

'I sincerely believe they do.'

Shimizu's eyes glistened. His voice was husky when he spoke again. 'Family is all I have.'

* * *

The next morning, Suzuki hailed Mihonoseki's sole taxi. The elderly driver wore a boat captain's hat and blue bow tie. While his nicotine-stained hands held the green Nissan Cedric mostly steady, she watched the land grow wilder and more beautiful. Camellias cast their red-yellow flowers across the winding road; mountain plum and loquat trees muscled for sunlight among the elms and dogwood. Through breaks in the forest, Suzuki caught glimpses of migratory birds in their hundreds riding the offshore swells, indifferent to plumes of spray that cast high on to the boulders.

When the taxi pulled into the Cape Mihonoseki lighthouse parking area, the driver's voice was raspy but kind. '660 yen, please,' he said.

The lighthouse stood at the very precipice of the cape—a brilliant white tower, sentinel-like beside the red-roofed keeper's quarters and observation station. At some stage, the latter had been reborn as Lighthouse Cafe. A sandwich board outside said it was open for lunch.

She took a seat at the window counter inside, and after consulting the menu, ordered the 'Fruits of the Sea' and a cold bottle of Kirin lager. Beyond the cliff tops and pulverizing swells below them, the Sea of Japan rolled on forever. A lone trawler boat bobbed like a cork, seagulls trailing in its wake. A ship's horn sounded and soon an enormous ferry slid from behind the cape and into view; its destination perhaps the Oki Islands whose languid blue forms drifted on the horizon.

Her meal arrived, arranged with the same meticulous attention to detail as it had the previous night at the Mihokan. Succulent slices of sashimi, scallops, oysters, and translucent squid, rested on a bed of glistening wakame, served with a cone of fresh wasabi and a small decanter of soy sauce.

As she ate, she ruminated over the bizarre events of the past twenty-four hours. After Shimizu had left her room, she'd telephoned his wife and family and given them the news. A weeping woman was a woman of few words—and Rumi Shimizu's tears did all the talking. What had surprised Suzuki most was the admission of the love affair, and without mentioning any names, the honourable decision was made to mutually end it for the benefit of all involved and the well-being of the family.

But, Danno?

It was not her business to speculate. And if he had been the secret lover, why had he recommended her to Rumi Shimizu? Guilt was not as strong a driver of human behaviour as the fear of public shame. To avoid an affair being made known, or worse—a divorce resulting from it—might have driven two lovers to a mutual agreement. Who was to know?

Suzuki had relayed the message that her husband had promised to call in the morning, and that all would be explained. Whether he did or not was none of her business. Her job was done, and she was exhausted.

After lunch she asked the staff to call the taxi, and while awaiting its arrival, followed the cliff-top path to the viewing platform beyond the lighthouse. The sea wind blew mightily, and she clutched her hat for fear of losing it on an updraft. At the tip of the peninsular, she peered down at the swells that thundered against the headland, the seabirds that glided effortlessly over them, and the yellow flowering succulents that clung stubbornly to the clifftops. She turned pensive. Humans were a lot like ocean swells; bundles of energy forever on the move, forever in a hurry, until some obstacle blocked their path and they would disintegrate in explosions of foam and spray, only to slip away and reconstitute, or reinvent themselves, before resuming their journey, bound for some other time and place.

A woman's voice reached her. From the cafe entrance the staff waved. The taxi had arrived.

Hurrying along the path, she glanced up in time to see Yukihiro Shimizu in his white uniform and a boat-shaped hat. He stood at the kitchen window, a towering lighthouse with its gaze fixed on some point far out to sea. It was a bittersweet irony that a man had had to run away in order to get closer to his family. She wondered what he was thinking.

* * *

Aboard the 'Swinging Yakumo', she reminded herself of one final task left to do. She opened the can of beer she had bought at the Matsue Station kiosk, slipped a spicy rice cracker into her mouth, and set up her laptop on the tray table. She took out the business card from her file and created a new email. She typed:

To the President of Fuji Freezer Systems,

I am writing to you from Matsue, Shimane Prefecture, where I have had the great misfortune to meet one of your employees, a Mr Junichiro Maeda, while travelling on business.

Mr Maeda's public drunkenness and lewd behaviour towards me in Matsue city were not only uncivilized, but extremely unbecoming of a salesman in your employ.

I strongly urge that some form of disciplinary action be taken against Mr Maeda to ensure this type of behaviour does not happen again.

I apologize for the tone of this letter but thank you for taking precious time to read it.

Yours sincerely,
M. Suzuki

Registered Private Investigator
Hyogo Prefecture

She addressed it to the public affairs department, whose email was listed on the company's website, and clicked 'send'.

Satisfied, she stowed her laptop and reclined her chair, happy in the knowledge that she had two more cans of beer to see her through to Okayama.

* * *

The last days of autumn passed in a flurry of work and family commitments. There was the annual sweet potato-digging trip to her daughter's school farm, the apartment tenants' meeting, the neighbourhood autumn festival, and most taxing of all, her mother's eye surgery to arrange. Thankfully, the fee from the Shimizu case covered the costs, and with a little help from neighbours and friends, she battled through the rest.

So, it was with great relief that she stepped off the train at Maiko seaside station and into the waning light of the last Sunday afternoon in November.

Teizo stood waiting on the other side of the ticket gate. With his faded jeans, windbreaker, and a threadbare baseball cap, his fisher fashion statement was complete. In his hands were two fishing rods and a tackle box. He had convinced her that if she wanted to witness a Kobe sunset, she may as well do it fishing.

Crossing the footbridge from the station, they walked shoulder to shoulder, unhurried, dwarfed by the massive columns of the Akashi Ohashi Bridge whose traffic shuttled back and forth between Honshu and Awaji Island in endless procession.

'So ... were the gods kind to you?' he asked, as they reached the esplanade.

'It's hard to say,' she said. 'You know I make my own luck, but sometimes a helping hand comes from nowhere to nudge things along.'

Though he said little, she knew he hungered for details. 'It's a long story,' she said at last. 'Too long for this autumn day.'

They arrived at the seaside pathway, which ran beneath the bridge and overlooked the sweeping currents of the Akashi Strait. Along its entire length, hobby fisherfolk lined the railings, casting into the swift-running tide.

They found a space between a young couple and an elderly fisher. Sensing Teizo's disappointment at her caginess, she pulled a small paper packet from her jacket pocket and held it out to him. 'I brought you something.'

He slipped out the red snapper amulet and a smile worked on to his chapped lips. 'Is this my helping hand?'

'Hot off the heavenly highway.'

'Well, what are we waiting for?'

He baited their hooks with slivers of squid and showed her how to cast her line without snagging fellow fisher folk. She'd never angled before in her life. Now, as she watched the DayGlo orange bobber rise and fall on the swell, she wondered why Teizo hadn't suggested this sooner. Perhaps he'd thought it below her station—a receptionist from a five-star hotel among old salts who cackled, smoked, and drank beer, guessing the destinations of the passing freighters and ferries that sailed into the sunset?

It mattered not. Her station felt just right.

All at once, Teizo gave a shout.

The fishing rod jerked in his hands, its line switching back and forth through the water. 'Grab the net!' he cried.

She dropped her rod and scrambled for the hand net.

Dog walkers and cyclists paused to spectate. Fellow anglers watched on with envy.

'Bravo!' she shouted, watching as Teizo hauled the fish slowly but surely towards him.

Up from the depths it came, glinting and gleaming, to burst into the last rays of autumn sunshine—a huge red snapper.

Sounds of the Tide

Spring arrived with all the usual excitement of new beginnings across the archipelago. Companies hired new recruits, children entered schools, and universities commenced the new academic year. To help things along, TV weather presenters donned pink jackets, towns slung plastic cherry blossoms from their eaves, and beverage makers masked their bottles and cans in sakura motifs.

The optimism, while short-lived, was infectious. That is to say, Suzuki had started her celebrations early.

Seated aboard the Special Rapid Express train, she now regretted having allowed Teizo to talk her into a second bottle of Chablis at Bar Bon Voyage the night before. She popped a mint into her mouth.

It had been an informal anniversary, one to mark that sunny day in late March two years ago, when she had stopped to admire the *Kaiwo Maru*, the four-masted sailing ship used for training naval cadets, which had moored alongside the Orient Hotel.

'She's a beauty isn't she?' a rich, smooth voice had sounded beside her. Suzuki turned to take in the handsome fifty-something with a tanned face and easy grin.

'I'm curious—why are ships referred to as women?'

'Goes back to the olden days when a ship was revered as a mother, a goddess, protecting the lives of the crew and all who sailed aboard her.'

'You believe that?'

'I'm alive, aren't I?'

It remained a source of humour between them; her accusing him of *nanpa*, picking up a younger woman, and he, in defence, claiming that conversation with an attractive middle-aged woman was far more exciting than landing a red snapper.

Now, two years on, she still found it hard to define their relationship. Were they boyfriend and girlfriend? Platonic pals? Barflies-in-arms? Or simply a pair of lost souls searching for life's meaning together? Laughter was a powerful aphrodisiac, but there were nights when she yearned for more than just playful jibing. Perhaps he did too?

Through the train window, Suzuki watched Kobe's seaside suburbs slide by in an unending sprawl. Small cities like Maiko, Akashi, Nishi Akashi, and Kakogawa came and went in a colourless chain of housing developments, shopping malls, and factories that had long since consumed the verdant green rice fields that once divided them.

She took out her phone and tapped on her photo collection, scrolling to the image that Sota Shimizu had sent her several months ago. It was a photo of the family standing before the Miho Taisha Shrine; Sota and Miku centred, both holding fishing rods, Rumi Shimizu to one side, Yukihiro and his half-sister, Yumiko, to the other. All of them were smiling.

The Shimizu case fee had been helpful, but the new school year now brought with it a fresh wave of costs: Aya's primary school gym clothes, requisite bag, new shoes, lunch fees, and advance payment for field trips. Adding to her concerns was the new Orient Hotel reception manager, Mr Goto. The hiring decision by the hotel directors had crushed any chance of a promotion she'd been hoping for, and along with it, a pay rise.

Then out of the blue, Rumi Shimizu had telephoned her. An acquaintance of hers wished to meet. No other information had been forthcoming, except the woman's name—Chiaki Yamamoto—and that she lived in Himeji city.

Suzuki popped another mint in her mouth, willing the light hangover away. As the train crossed the Ichi River and entered Himeji's outer limits, the sight she'd been anticipating came into view. Shirasagi-jo, the four-hundred-year-old samurai castle, loomed over the city's mishmash of architectural clumsiness as both a beacon to sightseers and symbol of enduring beauty to its citizens. Its pure white exterior resembled its namesake, the white egrets, which roosted in the paulownia trees beside the moat. Fortunate was the photographer who caught their graceful flight over the castle's tapered eaves at dawn or dusk.

Himeji was also her mother's hometown.

Thus, to visit was to travel back to her own childhood, recalling the stayovers at her grandmother's farmhouse on the slopes of Hiromine mountain, of falling asleep to cricket songs and waking to Obachan's singing and slices of chilled watermelon. The Kobe people, her grandmother used to say, regarded Himeji folk as unsophisticated and uncouth. 'Our rough dialect is fearsome when shouted in anger!' But Suzuki knew better. Himeji people were festival-loving folk, boisterous, kind, and hard-working.

It was for these reasons that she had found her brief conversation with Chiaki Yamamoto on the phone several days ago somewhat curious. The woman's manner had been refined, her words carefully chosen, her tone courteous if not slightly superior-sounding. She had sincerely apologized for asking Suzuki to make the trip to Himeji this Saturday morning. It was the only time she could meet.

Outside JR Himeji Station, Suzuki stepped into the brilliant noon light. Puffs of cumulus drifted like Zeppelins across the city. Despite the agreeable weather, February's temperature lingered and she had to walk briskly up Otemae-dori Street, the main thoroughfare, to fend off its chill. She passed kimono rental shops, confectionary stores, and souvenir stands busy with foreign sightseers. She paused outside an udon noodle restaurant to watch a man with powder-white hands rolling dough beside his steaming cauldron. He glanced up, and through the billows, smiled at her.

At the castle's main gate, she turned west and followed the willow-lined moat to the entrance to Kokoen Garden. After paying her entry fee, she took a winding path through a grove of the *sasa* bamboo and entered the main pavilion. A flowering bonsai plum tree greeted her in the foyer, its fragrance lingering in her nostrils long after she'd crossed over a covered bridge to an adjoining pavilion. This looked on to a carp-filled pond, around whose edges retinues of uniformed men perched on ladders, meticulously trimming and shaping the black and red pine trees. At the sign announcing, 'To Soju-an', she ducked beneath a low entranceway and soon arrived at the paved courtyard of a traditional tea house. It was the kind of journey one took in a fairy-tale book.

Suzuki supposed that Chiaki Yamamoto had chosen this teahouse for its peacefulness and privacy. On enquiring inside the foyer, however, she was surprised to hear the female staff use an honorific.

'I'm sorry, Yamamoto sensei is occupied at this moment. If you don't mind waiting, I will tell her that you are here. May I have your name please?'

'Mami Suzuki.'

She glanced about at the neat rows of shoes lining the shelves. Barely a murmur sounded from behind the *fusuma* sliding doors at the end of a long hallway.

Presently, a door slid sideways and a woman appeared. Her small, diminutive steps gave the impression of gliding rather than walking. Chiaki Yamamoto wasn't short, but her kimono of peach pink with a glimmering silver *obi* belt around which there were fastened braided cords of gold and red, lent her a doll-like quality. Her kohl black hair was fashioned into a tight coiffure that was both traditional and chic. Her make-up resembled that of a Shiseido model—luminous, mature, impeccable—and her slippers peeped like two white rabbits beneath the hem of her kimono. On reaching the genkan, she smiled graciously and bowed.

'Ms Suzuki, welcome to Soju-an. Thank you so much for coming all the way from Kobe.' Her smile never faded. 'I have instructed my students to continue without me. We are busy today, but they'll manage. Let's walk, shall we?'

'You're a *sado* teacher?'

She laughed lightly. Lifting a pair of pearl-coloured slippers from the shelf, she placed her tiny feet inside and said, 'I didn't tell you? I'm sorry. It is our school's turn to serve the visitors today.'

They departed the courtyard through a mouse-hole entrance at the rear and were soon strolling along a pathway lined with white oak and camphor trees, sunlight dappling the way ahead.

'Rumi Shimizu is an old school friend … in case you are wondering. We attended Kenmei High School together. We often meet for coffee when I'm in Kobe. I simply adore her Tiffany designs.'

Suzuki nodded politely. Kenmei was a private Catholic middle school for daughters of wealthy industrialists, bureaucrats, and doctors. Its reputation for teaching refinement and etiquette was well known. It was, she mused, rather an anomaly in a city like Himeji.

Where the path ended, they passed through a roofed gateway and into a garden of sculptured azalea bushes.

'Rumi tells me you are very thorough—and you are good with people. Those are qualities I respect.'

They arrived at a stream and followed its lazing course around a grove of maple trees. In places, steppingstones served as fords. Suzuki noted with both pleasure and surprise the giant red and white carp that swam fearlessly between them.

Beneath the tangle of an ancient wisteria vine, they seated themselves on a wooden bench. Chiaki Yamamoto clasped her hands together on her lap, and gazing into the stream, proceeded.

'You may feel that what I'm about to tell you is beyond your capabilities, beyond even human reasoning perhaps. But please hear me out, and please do not feel pressured by my proposition.'

'Of course.'

'On 28 March last year my brother, Kenjiro, died in a drowning incident. The police investigation determined it was accidental, although, they said, the consumption of alcohol had played a part. He was sixty-two years old. He died on his birthday.'

'I'm so sorry,' Suzuki said.

'There is another coincidence. Kenjiro had only just retired and had left Tokyo where he'd been working for forty years, to join his wife in Ishigaki.'

'Ishigakijima—in Okinawa?'

'A small town called Kabira, to be precise. His wife runs a guesthouse there.'

Thoughts leap-frogged through Suzuki's mind. She reined them in as Chiaki Yamamoto continued.

'I believe my brother's death was not accidental. That is the reason I asked you to meet me here today. I would like you to find out not what happened, but *how* it happened. I'm prepared to pay double what you charged Rumi Shimizu to do so.'

Concealing her surprise, Suzuki said evenly, 'I'm sorry, but I'm not qualified in forensics. I must also add ... I don't take on cases involving the death of family members. I'm not a criminologist.'

'I'm not seeking new facts about the cause of death. Those have been already ascertained. He died by drowning. Alcohol was involved. I accept that. Of course, my brother liked to drink. He often overdrank. But this, I believe, was to cope with the stress of his career. He ran an advertising agency in Harajuku. He was also physically capable—and he could swim.' Chiaki Yamamoto calmed herself and steadied her voice. 'I want to know how he drowned, and I'm prepared to pay for it.' Before Suzuki could respond, she added, 'Yes. Travel to Ishigaki will be required, but all expenses will be paid in full.'

Suzuki gazed at the stream. It arced peacefully around them. A small carp struggled at the stone ford, flapping its tail and splashing water as it tried to gain purchase in the current.

'Rumi Shimizu confided in me,' Chiaki Yamamoto continued. 'She told me that you were able to locate her husband and convince him to contact his family.'

'As a matter of fact, I didn't—'

'You have a special skill set. One that I have absolutely no doubt can be applied to my situation, and one which I am willing to pay for.'

'That's very kind of you but....'

'Do you mind if we take a short drive?'

'Right now?'

'It will only take about thirty minutes. There's someone I'd like you to meet.'

In the car park opposite the garden, the lights of a metallic green BMW 7-series blinked ahead of them. Chiaki Yamamoto painted a striking image as she lifted her kimono hem delicately and climbed behind its wheel. Moments later, her slippered feet edged the large saloon car into the westward flow of traffic heading out of the city. A few minutes later, she took a sharp left turn into a hillside side street, causing Suzuki's mind to churn. They were entering Nagoyama Cemetery.

At the top of the hill, the BMW pulled into the car park beside the tall white Buddhist pagoda. The city's suburbs disappeared into the fresh green of the western mountains. They descended through terraces of neat gravestones, stopping at a faucet for Chiaki Yamamoto to fill a steel bucket and take a ladle from the rack. Carefully, she made her way along a row of gravestones to a monolith of shining black granite. Kanji characters, inlaid with gold paint, read, *Miki Kazoku*, Miki Family. Fresh Easter lilies stood in receptacles either side.

'Would you mind?' Chiaki Yamamoto asked. 'I don't want to splash my kimono.'

'Of course,' said Suzuki, taking the bucket. She gently ladled water over the dark stone while Chiaki Yamamoto took a tube of candles and incense sticks from her purse. She lit two candles, then all the incense sticks. Stepping back, she clasped her hands and bowed.

'Kenjiro,' she said in a soft tone. 'This is Ms Suzuki. She has come to help us.'

Suzuki bowed.

'Kenjiro was my only brother. He was born and raised here. Himeji is where he belongs—with our mother and father.'

'His wife is Okinawan?'

'They met in Tokyo, married, but remained childless. She ran a restaurant there, but when her parents died, she returned to Ishigaki to take over her parents' guesthouse business.'

'May I ask what your primary suspicion is?'

'I've been seeing an *uranaishi*.' She glanced quickly at Suzuki, searching for judgement perhaps, but there was none. 'The uranaishi believes Kejiro's spirit is restless, that there is something it requires done. Something unfinished….'

'You suspect someone's involvement in his death?'

'His wife's.'

'On what grounds?'

'She had her reasons.' Chiaki Yamamoto grew flustered. 'Look, I will pay fifty per cent more if you can prove beyond a doubt that she was involved.'

'I assume your brother had taken out life insurance?'

'The company refused to pay. The coroner stated alcohol had contributed to his death.'

'Any other possible financial motive?'

'Kenjiro and I were close. We talked about his life in Ishigaki on the phone. He told me that he was enjoying his retirement but said his wife's business was failing. In our last conversation, he said he was trying to help her. Then, a month later he was dead.'

'Was he depressed?'

'As I said, he was enjoying life.'

Suzuki turned back to the grave. Incense smoke rose in purple tails, curling about the lilies before dissipating. 'What's your timeframe?'

'How soon can you begin?'

'Well, I'll need more information and time to consider….'

'Of course. There's a file in my car. It contains everything you need to get started—life insurance documents, newspaper articles, a police statement, and a copy of the coroner's report.'

'How did you get a coroner's report?'

'My husband is a surgeon at the Junkanki Prefectural Hospital. He used his connections.'

After bidding farewell to her brother with a short bow, Chiaki Yamamoto led Suzuki back up the path to the car.

'I do apologize,' she said, once seated behind the wheel. 'To ask you to go beyond what the police have already established may seem somewhat daunting.' She took from the rear seat a plastic file and passed it to Suzuki. 'I'm sure you have questions, but let's consider those once you have reviewed the documents.'

At this point in a meeting, Suzuki usually gave a prospective client a document of her own—her list of fees for service rendered. Given that Chiaki Yamamoto had put a generous offer on the table, it seemed redundant; the finer points of the contract could be ironed out later, should she decide to take the case.

The tea ceremony teacher revved the engine. 'Now, I will serve you tea,' she said. 'There is no better way to empty the mind of all clutter and to purge oneself of worries and concerns than to practise the way of tea. Will you accompany me back to Soju-an? I must check on my students.'

Suzuki felt drained yet could only manage, 'Certainly.' Chiaki Yamamoto was a persuasive woman; a velvet hammer, she might have said—one who gave the impression that she was an adept manager of her, as well as others', affairs.

The one thing that bothered Suzuki most was the uranaishi connection. Fortune tellers were bad news for private investigators. They were about as useful as a Groucho Marx disguise kit. They could hinder an investigation by confusing a client or causing them to make irrational demands based on 'voices from beyond the grave'. The only currency worth anything to a private eye was hard facts, the merit of which had to be weighed against a case's chance of success.

However, the uncomfortable truth was that money changed everything—and the pressing fact that she badly needed the work.

* * *

A short while later, seated at the edge of Soju-an's vast tatami floored salon, she watched as the last of the garden visitors departed and the young sado students moved about quietly, cleaning up.

When Chiaki Yamamoto appeared it was with a girl of about ten years of age, wearing a crimson and pink kimono with a lavender obi. As she padded carefully towards Suzuki with a tray in her hands, her tongue protruded with the effort of concentration. Slowly, she lowered herself to the floor and placed a dish containing a sweet *manju* rice cake in the shape of a cherry blossom in front of Suzuki. Next, a bowl of freshly whisked matcha green tea. Both server and receiver bowed. It was a moment when the innocence of youth confronted the wisdom of adulthood, when both girl and woman looked fleetingly into each other's eyes and saw something lost and something to be gained.

Teacher and student then left her alone to sample her manju and savour the green tea. Sweetness and bitterness, innocence and wisdom—did they not complement one another?

Chiaki Yamamoto returned a short while later to collect the dishes. Her movements were precise, measured, and as smooth as silk. 'I'd like to drive you back to Kobe, if you'll allow me,' she said, and before Suzuki could refuse, 'It's no trouble at all—I have an appointment at Ms Shimizu's showroom in Sannomiya this evening.'

A half hour later, the BMW's wide tyres gripped the highway heading east towards Osaka, the engine purring like a great cat stretching its legs. Chiaki Yamamoto was a sure-handed driver, relaxed and at ease behind the wheel, even if she did drive a little too fast. They glided between container trucks and airport buses, flew in and out of tunnels and across overpasses. Suzuki glanced at the speedometer—then decided not to.

'Do you know what my dream job was as a child?'

'Jet pilot?'

She laughed. 'I wanted to be a truck driver. I wanted to master a machine.' Her manicured fingers drummed on the leather steering wheel. 'Before this, I owned a Hummer H2, but my husband pressured me to sell it. What kind of tea ceremony teacher drives a six-thousand cc SUV to a teahouse? He was right, parking is terrible.'

The Rokko mountains loomed before them and soon the honeycombed strata of suburban Kobe slipped into view.

Suzuki took a deep breath. It was now or never. 'To be honest,' she began, 'this matter of your brother's drowning may be a little too much for me to take on. I have family commitments that prevent me from travelling too far afield—at least, for the time and distance this case will require.'

'Then take your family along.'

'Pardon me?'

'How many in your family?'

'Three—including myself.'

'Then take them with you. A family visiting Ishigaki is far more natural. You won't raise any suspicions.'

Suzuki's gaze swung back to the road. Mother and daughter on a plane to a small island at the very bottom of Japan? That would be a first.

'I will cover expenses for all three of you,' Chiaki Yamamoto said. 'I only ask that you stay in Kabira at the guesthouse of my brother's wife. You will find those details in the file.'

Madness? Yes, it was. But the longer Suzuki pondered it, the less crazy it seemed. She had a week of holidays owing to her in mid-April, and she was obliged to take them, as the hotel needed all staff for the national Golden Week holidays beginning at the end of April. She had been thinking of Kinosaki Onsen, a night in a ryokan with a crab dinner and a hot spring bath. Other than that, she hadn't considered the remaining days.

Holidays were expensive. A working holiday, on the other hand ... was that doable?

She politely requested to be dropped off at the train station closest to her home. As the big green BMW rolled to a stop, Chiaki Yamamoto turned to her. 'Thank you for meeting with me today.' She touched Suzuki's arm lightly and her gaze was sincere. 'Please do telephone me if you have any questions. I'm looking forward to our next contact.'

Suzuki thanked her and asked that she pass on her regards to Rumi Shimizu. The smile came with a rev; then the petite tea ceremony teacher in the apricot kimono pulled away from the curb and melted into the eastward-flowing traffic.

* * *

After a dinner of *mizutaki-nabe*—hot pot crammed with Chinese cabbage, tofu, udon, and cheap pork cuts—Suzuki cleared the table while her mother and daughter migrated to the living room to laugh at a rerun of the TV comedy, *Yoshimoto-Shinkigeki*.

She poured herself a glass of convenience store wine—Chilean Chardonnay was the best value for money—then gathered her ageing laptop and files and sat down at the kitchen table.

Chiaki Yamamoto was a thorough woman. The file contained no less than a dozen documents, meticulously notated in neat, cursive handwriting, which gave it the feel of a school project by an A-seeking student.

Deep down in her mind, a warning light flicked on. Obsessiveness could be dangerous in the driver's seat. Should a client expect a certain outcome, their willingness to accept anything different might result in a major headache for the private investigator. Chiaki Yamamoto did not seem the type to renege on a deal just because the facts might displease her, but there was a first-time for everything.

She viewed the newspaper reports first. There were two articles, both short and pointed, like those dedicated to traffic accidents and shipping mishaps. From the *Ishigaki Shimbun* the headline read '62-year-old man drowns in Kabira Bay'; from the *Ryukyu Shimpo*, 'Body of retiree recovered from pearl farm'.

Suzuki made notes and then turned to her browser. A search revealed the existence of a pearl-farming operation in Kabira Bay; not standard pearls but the rare black kind, cultured inside black-lipped oysters and farmed only in Tahiti and the Yaeyama Islands of southern Japan.

The *Ishigaki Shimbun* reported that the body of Kenjiro Miki, 62, had been discovered at around 6.30 p.m. on 29 March. The *Ryukyu Shimpo* added that the body had been discovered by an employee of Kabira Pearls Ltd. during a routine check of the nurseries and that divers from the Ishigaki Fire Department had retrieved it soon after.

Suzuki brought up a map of Kabira, a township that comprised two clusters—one at the mouth of Kabira Bay and the other a short distance further along the coast. Two narrow inlets connected the bay to the ocean, flowing on either side of Kojima, an uninhabited island that acted as a natural barrier to the sea. She assumed that this sheltered location, with its regular tidal movements, made Kabira Bay an ideal place for pearl farming.

She took a sip of Chardonnay and moved on to the police and coroner's reports, wondering what kind of influence Chiaki Yamamoto's husband had wielded to acquire them. The police report was a standard procedural form, clinical and impersonal, with details typed into boxes like those on a driving licence application.

The Ishigaki Coroner's Office yielded more. Kenjiro Miki's body had shown no physical signs of violence. Abrasions to his arms and legs were 'likely due to contact with coral on the seafloor'. Welts on his face and neck were determined to be the result of jellyfish stings, although they were 'not consistent with those of the *habu-kurage* box jellyfish', and deemed to be fatal. A blood test showed no toxins but confirmed a blood alcohol concentration reading of 0.15.

0.15.

It would require hours of steady drinking, or a shorter period of intense consumption, to achieve such a reading in an adult male. Chiaki Yamamoto had said her brother enjoyed a drink—it *was* his birthday after all. The universally accepted definition of 'drunk' was 0.08 per cent BAC, but this wasn't useful when deciding an individual's capacity to function mentally and physically, simply because some people were better at holding their drink than others. The official record stated that Kenjiro Miki, aged sixty-two, of Kabira, had died of pulmonary oedema resulting from a saltwater drowning. No suspicious circumstances were found to have caused, or 'helped to cause', this outcome.

Her gaze lingered over the words, 'helped to cause'.

If Chiaki Yamamoto suspected her brother's wife's hand in the death, that is where her investigation would focus. But how on earth could a wife 'cause' her husband—a capable swimmer according to his sister—to get so tanked as to drown in an inlet considered placid enough for pearl farming?

She bulleted her questions, drained her glass, and poured another. She turned to the page to a colour printout of the Yadokari Guesthouse. The description read:

Rest and rejuvenate in traditional Okinawan surroundings at Yadokari Guesthouse. Situated only minutes from the warm clear waters of Kabira Bay.

We have been accommodating guests for over forty years and serving authentic home cooking with true Okinawan hospitality. All our rooms are traditional style with air-conditioning and window bay views. We are only a ten-minute walk from pub-restaurants, gift shops, and Kabira Beach where you can enjoy glass-bottom boat tours, beach walks, and shell collecting.

Suzuki studied the pamphlet with the image of a woman standing behind a reception desk. She looked to be in her late fifties, but the poor resolution of the image made it difficult to discern anything more.

She turned to the last pocket of the file. It contained a single photo—a studio wedding portrait—and it had not been placed there as an afterthought. Rather, it served as a visual underscore, the final piece in Chiaki Yamamoto's package: a man and a woman, unsmiling but not unhappy, staring at the camera. Penned beneath, 'Kazuha' and 'Kenjiro'. It had been a traditional Shinto wedding: the groom replete in *hakama*, the bride swathed in white kimono with a *tsunokakushi* headdress over the topknot of her *bunkin takashimada*-style wig. It was said to veil the bride's 'horns of jealousy', ego, and selfishness, and to demonstrate the bride's intent to become a gentle and obedient wife.

Suzuki flipped back a page, comparing the two faces: the same woman in different places, different eras. Had married life changed her for better or for worse?

A voice called from the living room. 'Aya's asleep,' said her mother drowsily.

Suzuki glanced at the clock, surprised that almost two hours had elapsed since she'd opened the file. She rose from the table, entered the cosy living room and lifted her daughter from the small sofa. It was a Houdini act, undressing a limp child and putting them in pyjamas, for which a knowledge of body mechanics greatly assisted. Teeth-cleaning, on the other hand, could wait till the morning.

When she returned to the kitchen, the TV channel had changed. Sounds of a comedy duo wafted in from the living room where a *tsukkomi*, a straight-faced comedian, and his *boke*, the funny guy, kept up a machine-gun commentary on the merits of sleeping in commuter trains.

Suzuki poured out the last of the wine and checked airline tickets for two adults and one child to Ishigaki Island. She compared hire car rates, and finally the Yadokari Guesthouse tariff. After calculating extra for daily expenses, she arrived at a round figure for a three-night trip—it came to a little more than her monthly salary.

She leant back in her chair, half-listening to the comedy duo's routine accompanied by audience laughter and her mother's quiet chuckles. If she and Teizo were a comedy team, who would be the straight-talker and who would be the joker? The thought amused her. Perhaps they were a little of both.

Teizo and Mami the straight-talkers, Teizo and Mami the funny guys. Making each other laugh was a team effort.

She reached for her phone.

* * *

They met at a small Indian restaurant with a blue door on a side street just a few minutes' walk from Motomachi Station. It was a place where Teizo occasionally dined with his fisher friends. The dishes were colourful and sumptuous, the spiciness just right.

Afterwards, they strolled south through Chinatown, but rather than stopping in at Bar Bon Voyage, they continued into the financial district. If she considered herself a private investigator, then Teizo was a nightspot gumshoe. The bar's name was Ember Days, and it occupied the first-floor of a Taisho-era building across the street from Nippon Bank's Kobe headquarters. Lamps glowed at its window tables and a sign board outside announced the night's jazz offerings.

The regular crowd was in, but Teizo knew the owner, a former Coast Guard pilot who loved bebop and jazz, and who had reserved two seats for them at the end of the antique wood counter.

'I didn't know you liked jazz,' she said.

'I don't really, but this place reminds me of San Francisco. We used to dock there in the seventies. How about a rusty nail?'

Teizo never talked much about his life as a submariner for the Japan Self-Defense Forces, except after a few drinks, and even then it was in a sweeping philosophical sense—about the sea, survival, freedom, and travel—or to draw comparisons between life at sea and life on the land. She never asked for more than he cared to offer, and he never asked her too many questions or gave her advice unless she asked for it. He kept his private life to himself—as she did her own. She was sure there was lots to tell but tears would flow telling it, and tonight was neither the time nor the place.

'So…' he said, watching the bow-tied mixologist set to work. 'I feel a mystery brewing?'

The barman laid the cocktails before them with a flourish.

'Kanpai,' she said, touching her glass to his own and taking a sip. He sat, watching her intently.

'Alright, Watson. Here it is,' she said finally. 'Here's what's bothering me. A client—a *potential* client—who believes they have the answer to their problem but wants me to prove it for them.'

'Is Tokai Pearls knocking?'

'Couldn't be more different. The client is taking their cue from an uranaishi.'

Teizo chuckled and shook his head.

'What? Teizo, a nonbeliever?'

'The only fortune I believe is the one I tell myself each morning when I wake up.'

'Which is?'

'Today is your lucky day.'

'Seriously, what's your opinion?'

'Of uranaishi? They take your money and tell you what you want to hear. They're psychologists, salespeople of the spirit world. They start broad, with things that have happened to ninety per cent of us—an accident, a sibling in trouble, a job change, a recently deceased relative … and they watch for signs, for body language, for affirmation of truth. Then they exploit it.'

'You're preaching to the converted. But why would a wealthy, educated woman, married to a doctor, believe an uranaishi who says that her deceased brother's spirit is restless?'

'Of course he's restless! All cooped up in an urn for the rest of his days. Not for me, No ma'am—my ashes will be scattered over the sea.'

'To become fish food and possibly supper for some innocent like me.'

'To answer your question, you may be dealing with a woman who is less at peace than her brother.'

Suzuki turned back to the bar. Gazing at the bottles of exotic liquor, glowing against the shelf lamplights, she said glumly, 'I was afraid you'd say that.' She swallowed her drink. 'How about an *awamori*?'

'You sure?'

'I'm in training.'

'For what?'

'Ishigaki Island.'

He looked at her incredulously.

'A small town called Kabira, to be exact. You know it?'

'As a matter of fact, I do,' he said, his tone suddenly enthusiastic. 'I've scuba-dived there. Back in the eighties with my SDF friends.'

'Pray, do tell.'

'What do you want to know? It's a tourist town with a beautiful bay where nothing much happens.'

'Pearl farming happens.'

'It does—black pearls. And it's one of the best manta-viewing spots in the world. There's a channel off its coast ... but if you're not a diver, there's nothing much else.'

'There's a beach.'

'You can't swim there.'

'Jellyfish?'

'The tidal currents are too strong.' He levelled his gaze with hers. 'What do uranaishi, rich women with a dead brother, and Okinawa all add up to?'

'That,' she sighed, 'is the question that kept me awake last night.'

An amplifier whined and a microphone burst into life behind them. A female vocalist in a black one-piece dress stepped into the light, thanking the patrons. Then a drummer and a double bassist led her into the first song.

Teizo ordered cocktails of *awamori*—the fiery Okinawan spirit fermented from Thai rice—mixed with guava juice and served with a golden slice of *shiikuwāsā* lime.

It wasn't long before a new sensation overcame her, as if her head had somehow detached itself from her body and was now threatening to float away. It was not an unpleasant feeling. In fact, it was *very* pleasant. The bee-bop beat, the awamori, and the low-lit bar with its affable mixologist, all conspiring to set her adrift. A wonderful numbness enveloped her, as if the world suddenly had no hard surfaces or sharp corners. The table lamps glowed like fat cocoons. The vocalist's lips glistened, her notes soaring and plunging before melting into the dimness.

Teizo's lips moved but she heard nothing. She leant in close, close enough to smell guava on his breath. He spoke into her ear, and whatever it was he said tickled. She laughed out loud. She rested her head on his shoulder, her eyelids no longer able to defy gravity.

The audience applauded. The singer thanked the room. Suzuki roused herself and called the barman for iced water. Tomorrow would bring a new day, one she hoped wouldn't begin with a hangover. She had three suitcases to pack.

* * *

From the window of Peach Air flight MM231, Suzuki looked on to the crisp columns of altocumulus rising over the Philippine Sea. A cargo ship slid in and out of view, sailing towards Taiwan. The flight map above her tray table showed the island of Miyakojima ahead, signalling their approach to the Yaeyama-shoto, a clutch of islands resembling a disintegrating meteorite that had broken loose from Kyushu. At its centre lay the guitar-shaped island of Ishigakijima, the administrative centre of the Yaeyamas, and their destination. It occurred to her that she was now closer to Taipei than to Tokyo.

Aya slept.

In the seat beside her daughter, her mother fiddled with the entertainment system panel. She'd been doing so ever since take-off, and it had now began to grate on Suzuki's nerves.

Deep down she knew self-doubt was making her irritable; not over whether her mother and daughter would enjoy themselves—that was the easy part—but about the business arrangement with Chiaki Yamamoto. For the first time in her short career as a private eye, she felt out of her depth. The generous up-front payment had sealed the deal and now obliged her to furnish results. What weighed on her most was the fact that a man had died and the cause of his death had been established. She could well be searching for something that didn't exist.

Could a widow who had known her husband's life insurance company would not pay in the event of a death due to alcohol consumption—maliciously or recklessly—have caused his death? According to Chiaki Yamamoto, she would be receiving a monthly retirement payment from his company, but Suzuki knew that this often amounted to little more than what the National Pension Fund paid. What other triggers might there have been? Domestic violence? Psychological abuse? A secret mistress? Teizo's words returned to her: *You may be dealing with a woman who is less at peace than her brother.*

Could it be that Chiaki Yamamoto was hearing voices?

She felt a hand on her arm and flinched.

'Are we there yet?' Aya asked.

Suzuki gazed down at her drowsy child. 'Almost there', she replied, watching the child's eyes close once more.

She asked the cabin attendant for a cup of coffee for herself and her mother, and then her gaze returned to the world beyond the window. A fleet of fishing boats appeared, then islets of emerald green ringed by white sand came into view, and finally a lumpy, formless land of plantations and pastureland, rimmed by a lagoon and an outer reef that separated it from the cobalt blue sea.

An Okinawan ballad drifted from the cabin speakers as the plane, bucking gently on the thermals, began its descent to Ishigaki Island.

'Where are my glasses?' her mother said.

'I feel sick,' moaned Aya.

The plane flew over the reef, the mangroves, and the town proper—so low that Suzuki could make out the face of a cyclist gazing up at her, an elderly man in a red shirt and with a shock of white hair standing on his brown head.

Rubber squealed on hot tarmac. The runway was short, and the wing flaps stood almost upright as fields of sugarcane flashed by in a green blur. Suzuki strained in her seat belt.

Aya vomited.

Her mother gripped the arm rests. When the plane eased to a halt, she cried, 'I found my glasses'—in her hand, a flattened frame with one lens missing—'I was sitting on them!'

It wasn't an auspicious start. Nevertheless, Suzuki cleaned her daughter's dress as best she could, pocketed her mother's broken glasses, and shepherded them out of the plane, down the gangway, and across the steaming runaway to the arrivals hall. The air was thick and moist, and heavy with the fragrance of the tropics. The disembarking passengers gulped at it like fish out of water.

The hired car was a sky-blue Nissan Note, and after she had bundled their baggage inside, confirming that everyone and everything was secured and accounted for, she programmed its navigation system with the address that the nice staff had given her. First stop: Tamura Eyeglasses.

* * *

Downtown Ishigaki shuffled to a far slower beat than Kobe. Traffic drifted, people ambled, and even the town clock was in no hurry, stuck at ten past seven. Between the typhoon-proof concrete buildings, traditional houses peered from behind voluminous bougainvillaea, hibiscus bushes, and bleached coral rock walls called *ishigaki*—the island's namesake. Pedestrians coloured the sidewalks with their floral motif shirts and dresses, carrying shopping bags of fruit and vegetables, and mysterious packages wrapped in newspaper. Everything was bright, cheerful, and deliciously simple. Suzuki felt her city skin begin to slip away.

Inside Tamura Eyeglasses, the staff, uniformed in pink and white shirts of hibiscus designs, were polite and spoke quietly, unlike the boisterous Kansai folk with their loud quips and guffawing. Within the hour, they had the repaired glasses in hand.

Back in the car, Suzuki studied the map and confirmed their route. It was a simple matter of following the coastline. There was just one idiosyncrasy: the map showed Yadokari Guesthouse by a different name, the Seabreeze Inn.

On the outskirts of the town, they stopped at a supermarket for snacks and drinks. A short while later, as they cruised down the coastal highway, her mother unwrapped a spam and egg rice ball. 'Delicious!' she said with her mouth full. Suzuki lowered the windows.

It was a rural idyll in the middle of the ocean. They passed by tractors ploughing dark soil with orange-necked herons feeding in their wake, cane fields where tired men sat in the shade of their trucks drinking out of glass bottles, mango trees and market gardens, grazing cattle with small birds perched on their rumps beneath a blazing sun, all so strange and foreign.

The road veered towards the coast, dipping in and out of coves and estuaries where mangrove trees grew in dark thickets and dinghies wallowed in mud. Save for the odd cyclist, a tour bus, and the occasional farm truck, the highway was theirs.

Aya vomited. Again.

On a roadside shoulder, Suzuki pulled over to clean up. A small truck sat parked nearby with a yellow parasol and a sign touting, 'Fresh Juice!' She strolled over and bought three mango smoothies.

'From Ishigaki?' she asked the young vendor in the battered straw hat.

'Kabira, actually,' he replied.

'Is it far?'

'Not far. Are you making a daytrip?'

'We're staying the night.' She slurped at her smoothie. 'At Yadokari Guesthouse. You know it?'

'Certainly do. The owner cooks real Okinawan dishes.'

'What are they like?'

'Very tasty.'

'I mean, the owner.'

The man's gaze leapt out to sea, then back to her. 'She's a nice woman,' he said.

They continued along the highway, her daughter and mother stifling yawns, and Suzuki, feeling the contagion, trying to stay alert. The road switched inland and climbed a forested hill. Daylight dimmed and everywhere the flora loomed large and riotous. A giant strangler fig tree with cascading aerial roots, palms as big as umbrellas, and flowers—azaleas of intense red, hibiscus of pink and orange, snow white lilies—all bowed in the small car's slipstream.

'Shit!'

She braked sharply.

Her mother lurched awake, eyes wide.

They looked on in disbelief as a small man in cut-off trousers, naked to the waist, stepped into the centre of the road holding a rope. Attached to the rope was a nose ring and attached to that was an enormous water buffalo. He waved an apology to Suzuki, led the beast across the road and vanished into the foliage on the other side.

'Everything here is big,' said her mother, breathing out. She reached for another spam and egg rice ball.

'Including your appetite,' said Suzuki, winding down the window again.

The two women laughed out loud.

* * *

The Kabira township lay on the windward side of the hill. As shown on the map, it was a town divided—one part clustered at the inlet, the other nestled on the far side of the bay. The highway descended into a shady tunnel of strangler figs at the bottom of which a sign indicated the turn-off to Kabira Beach. Suzuki wheeled left.

Houses appeared, raised on stilts with sliding wood doors and tiled roofs; some others were more modern, built of concrete and bunker-like. Kabira exuded a sleepy rundown feel, as if appearances did not matter and nature was best left to its own devices. A billy goat stood peering over a coral rock wall, chewing something as it watched them pass.

They descended through a leafy neighbourhood and at the very bottom of a laneway, they halted.

'Is that our hotel?' asked her daughter, peering between the seats.

All three women craned their necks and looked at the two-storied building with a rustic façade the colour of French vanilla and a tall palm tree growing out front. A traditional Okinawan residence, half-hidden by fruit trees, stood nearby.

'It is,' responded Suzuki.

A path led to a shady forecourt where, over the entranceway, a wooden plaque in calligraphic characters read 'Yadokari Inn'. A large hermit crab scuttled behind an earthen jar as they made their way up it. The sound of running water seemed to be everywhere.

'Gomen-kudasai! Hello?' Suzuki called inside the foyer.

In a few moments, a figure appeared in the hallway. Backlit by light of the window, it approached with slippered footsteps that set the smooth floorboards creaking.

'The Suzuki family?' it said. Then, a woman stepped into the light and smiled broadly. 'Welcome to Yadokari Guesthouse. My name is Kazuha Aragaki.'

Two things struck Suzuki immediately: the woman had reverted to her maiden name and she looked strong. Her arms were toned and tanned, her legs supple-looking and smooth, and her gleaming complexion gave her a look of indeterminable age. Which made perfect sense. Okinawa beat the rest of the country hands down in the longevity stakes; its low-fat diet, active lifestyle, and vigorous social life meant most islanders lived to be ninety or older. Suzuki wondered how long it would take a city woman like herself to achieve such a healthy, graceful look.

Aragaki led them up the stairs to the second-floor. On opening the door to their room, Suzuki's mother and daughter yelped with delight and ran to the window. The entire inlet to the bay lay before them—a sandy white beach lined with tour boats, a deep channel of intense turquoise-blue, and the verdant green Kojima Island surrounded by the shifting tide of the bay itself.

Suzuki peered down. A deck with chairs and tables faced the water, shaded by the broad fronds of two Yaeyama palms. At the far end of the deck, a grove of papaya trees stood heavy with fruit.

'Is it low tide?' she asked.

'Yes, it is,' Aragaki replied. 'It's a good time for gathering clams.' She glanced at the fidgeting child and restless grandmother. 'Would you like to join me clam hunting? I'll be serving them for dinner.'

'That's a fine offer, thank you,' said Suzuki. 'But I think we might take a stroll to stretch our legs. Will it still stand for tomorrow?'

'Of course.' Aragaki smiled. 'Dinner will be served downstairs at 6 p.m.'

Suzuki looked back at the channel. A slip of sand appeared just off the shore, sugar white and shimmering. 'Can we walk to that island?'

'The sandbar?' Aragaki joined her at the window, so close that Suzuki could smell her citrus fragrance. 'No—the current running through that channel is too strong to cross.'

'How about the beach?'

Aragaki wore a sympathetic expression. 'I'm sorry to say that swimming is prohibited because of the pearl farm.' She pointed to the far side of the bay where a natural bottle neck formed between Kojima Island and the coast, and hundreds of buoys floated in a grid-like pattern across its surface.

'Why not try Yonehara Beach? It's only a short drive along the coast. Seeing that you'll be staying for three days, you can visit anytime.'

Suzuki looked at the hot, puffy faces of her mother and daughter. The idea was a good one. Only, it would take her away from her field of investigation.

Perhaps sensing the change of mood, Aragaki said, 'Would you like me to launder your daughter's dress? I have to do another load anyway, so it's no trouble at all. Just drop it at reception on your way out.'

'That's very kind of you,' said Suzuki.

'I like her perfume,' said her mother when Aragaki had left the room.

Suzuki sighed.

It wasn't only the woman's scent that was likeable; her entire demeanour was disarming, so unlike Suzuki's over-zealous colleagues at the Orient Hotel who jumped at the slightest request from guests, as if their lives depended on it. A five-star hotel and a beachside guest house were different universes. Yet, the management of both sought the same goal—customer satisfaction.

The climate difference too was remarkable. Whereas Kobe had been chilly with sporadic rain showers and bursts of sunshine earlier that morning, Ishigaki's skies stretched clear and cloudless. The temperature hovered in the balmy high-twenties.

In the fragrant heat of the late afternoon, the three women ascended the narrow laneway, pausing at a small playground to let Aya stretch her legs. It afforded them an unobstructed view of Kabira Beach, the channel with its sand bar and Kojima Island beyond. There was the usual assortment of swings, see-saws, and a sandbox. Only one other child, a girl several years older than Aya wearing grubby gym clothes and a primary schooler's yellow cap, sailed back and forth on one of the swings. They exchanged greetings and soon the grandmother was sending her granddaughter back and forth with laughter and squeals.

'How was school today?' Suzuki asked the girl.

'Fun,' she replied. Her missing front tooth caused her words to whistle.

'Do you live here?'

'Over there.' She pointed to a block of weathered-stained concrete apartments set back from the laneway.

'Come here often?'

'Every day. Others, too. But I'm always early.'

'Why's that?'

'I do my homework as soon as I get home.'

Suzuki chuckled. 'I wished I'd been like you when I was a girl.' She gazed out at the bay. 'Such a great view. Too bad you can't swim.'

'Some people do.'

'Oh?'

'You're not allowed to, but they do.'

'Who does?'

'People.'

'Tourists?'

The girl nodded and her swing slowed.

'You've seen them?' asked Suzuki.

She nodded again. 'But the boatmen get angry.'

'Because of the pearl farm?'

She shook her head. 'It's dangerous.'

'Pee!' Aya cried, leaping off the swing and dancing about. 'Gotta go pee!'

By the time they had returned from the guesthouse bathroom, the playground resounded with the shouting and laughter of other neighbourhood children. Suzuki spied the young girl and waved.

They wandered along the main road into town, passing by a mini market, outside of which an elderly woman busied herself cutting pineapple with a cleaver on a wooden block. She offered them a sample of the sweetest pineapple they had ever tasted. Suzuki promised to buy some on their return.

They continued on, passing shops with 'OPEN' signs on their doors and dim, lifeless interiors. Suzuki assumed that would all change at month's end when the entire nation went on holiday and Golden Week began in earnest.

Kabira had a grocery store, gasoline station, post office, cafe, and a 'tourist trap' in the form of purpose-built emporium whose windows were cluttered with cheesy driftwood sculptures, clam shells, vials of star sand, and jewellery made from polished coral.

But what caught her attention was the warehouse at the town's centre. It was a large, dank-looking wooden building with wide-open doors and a dark, cavernous interior. Steam drifted from large wooden vats inside the door, redolent of cooked rice. The mystery was solved when they turned the corner. 'Omoto Awamori Brewery Ltd.' announced itself in expansive cerulean blue and gold lettering.

Further on, a row of tour boat ticket shacks lined the street. Beyond these, a sandy boardwalk led through the casuarina trees and down to the beach. In a few moments, the three women had shed their sandals and were running, laughing, and giggling across the powdery sand to the water's edge. The last of the tour boats was returning and Suzuki watched as its deckhands cast their mooring lines into waiting hands on the shore, lowered its gangplank, and helped passengers disembark without wetting a foot.

She noted the signs, erected at regular intervals along the high tide mark, warning beachgoers that swimming was strictly prohibited.

While grandmother and granddaughter set about collecting shells, Suzuki stepped to the water's edge to cool her feet. Kabira Beach was postcard perfect. That such a malicious act could take place in this paradise was hard to imagine. Doubly so, that a gracious host single-handedly running her own guesthouse in a sleepy seaside town should be the subject of her investigation. As the tide lapped at her ankles, she frowned. Finding a message in a bottle seemed more likely here.

Questions swam in circles in her mind. If Kenjiro Miki had lived in Kabira for almost six months, wouldn't he be aware of the dangers of swimming in the inlet, regardless of whether his wife had told him so or not? The signs were clearly visible.

This forced her to consider an unlikely possibility—that he had *wanted* to die. Although Chiaki Yamamoto had been adamant about her brother's stable mental health, and had even said that he was happy, Suzuki knew that few family members spoke without fear of public shame when *jisatsu*, or suicide, was involved. Blood would always be thicker than water.

Kenjiro Miki had been director of a busy Harajuku advertising agency. From big city boss to island retiree was quite a leap. Not everyone could handle such a seismic shift in lifestyle—Okinawa was not Tokyo. Japan's sunniest prefecture was also its poorest; the minimum hourly wage was just 792 yen and job opportunities were slim. The nation's corporate empires were mostly headquartered on Honshu, not to mention its best universities, sports teams, pop groups, and amusement parks. A tropical island was a nice place to live until it wasn't.

There was also the alcohol factor. Kenjiro Miki had liked to drink. A retired executive in a small island town with its own awamori brewery—that, itself, could be a slippery slope. But what bothered her most was that the one person who would know the answers, was the one she couldn't ask.

Not yet anyway.

As the tour boat crew tidied the decks and stowed the lifejackets for another day, she noted a subtle change in the flow of the channel water. The current now moved more swiftly than before, almost river-like, as it pushed in from the sea and entered the bay. It was time to return to the guesthouse.

The mini market was still open, but the elderly pineapple cutter was nowhere to be seen, and Suzuki decided to return another time. The shell hunting expedition had yielded a large cache, but under her orders the colourful midden was to be left at the guesthouse steps for sorting and cleaning the next morning.

Inside the foyer, a set of fearsome fish jaws hung over the door. She hadn't noticed them before. Reaching up, she ran her fingers over the needle-like teeth and their sharpness surprised her.

'Barracuda.'

The voice made her jump.

She wheeled around to find Aragaki smiling warmly at her. There had been no sound of creaking floorboards.

'My father caught that fish many years ago.' She laughed lightly. 'Don't worry, barracuda isn't on the menu tonight.'

Once again, Suzuki found herself having to recalibrate her senses, trying to reconcile this kindly soft-spoken woman with Chiaki Yamamoto's image of a scheming and disloyal wife.

'Why don't you come through to the deck,' Aragaki said. 'Dinner will be served soon, and you can enjoy a drink beforehand.'

'Wonderful. Do you serve Omoto awamori?'

'You saw the brewery? Kabira's one and only. They even have customers in Kyoto and Tokyo, you know.'

To a chorus of contented slurps and burps—grandmother and granddaughter clutching glasses of cool jasmine tea— Suzuki held her earthen cup of ice, water, and rice spirit to the setting sun and quietly thanked the gods for getting her through the day. Aided by this smooth tonic, the trials and tribulations of their first day in Okinawa were soon relegated to history.

With the tide having reached its zenith, Kabira Bay lay languid and serene before her; the only sign of life was a lone sea kayaker drifting through the inlet.

Through the opened doors of the dining room delicious aromas drifted, and presently, Aragaki called them to feast.

'You're my only guests until Wednesday,' she said, directing the three hungry women to a long wooden table inside. At each setting lay a myriad of small dishes: *umi-budo* sea grapes, pan-fried tuna cuts, reef fish sashimi, stir-fried bitter *goya* melon with tofu and bonito flakes, sesame tofu topped with tiny fish, pork belly simmered in brown sugar and soy sauce, steamed rice, and miso soup with clams.

'Crayfish!' cried her mother, lifting the lid on a small earthen pot.

'Actually, it's *yashigani*—coconut crab in a bonito broth,' said Aragaki. 'My cousin catches them in the mangroves on the other side of the bay.'

'Is Kabira your hometown?' Suzuki asked.

'I grew up here. The house on the other side of the orchard was built by my father.'

'And your parents still live here?'

'They passed away two years ago.'

'I'm sorry.'

As Aragaki set the last of the dishes down, she paused a moment. Her gaze fell to Suzuki's mother, happily tucking into the hot pot, and she seemed to regard the elderly woman with a sudden sentimental fondness. 'They would both have been in their nineties now,' she said. The words sounded faraway and meant only for herself.

'Okinawans are famed for their long lives.'

'They both died in a road accident.'

'Oh no.' Suzuki laid down her chopsticks.

'They were hit by a drunken cane truck driver.'

Suzuki said nothing.

Aragaki drew a sharp breath. 'I'm sorry,' she said, exhaling. 'You didn't need to hear all that.'

'It's quite alright,' Suzuki said. 'I'm very sorry for your loss ... we never know what lies around life's corners, do we?'

* * *

The sky had turned a deep bronze and the hills on the other side of the bay now resembled a row of dimpled, overturned saucepans. The three women returned to the deck to take in the cooler air and rest their stomachs. Only the quiet murmur of the lapping tide drifted up through the papaya trees.

'What are those?' Aya asked.

Suzuki followed her daughter's skyward gaze. 'Some kind of bird, I guess.'

'They're fruit bats,' called Aragaki through the dining room door. 'They roost in the hills but come down to the mangroves at night to eat insects.' She appeared carrying a dish of sliced pineapple which she placed on the deck table. Suzuki's mother tasted a piece. 'Fabulous! It's just like the pineapple from the corner store,' she exclaimed.

Aragaki laughed. 'It is. That's my elder sister's shop.'

'Your sister lives here, too?' said Suzuki.

'Just down the road. There are quite a few of us.'

'Have you lived here all your life?'

'No. I lived in Tokyo for many years after I married. My husband worked for a company, and I opened a small restaurant in Shinjuku's Omoide Yokocho, Memory Lane.'

'Okinawan food?'

'It was very popular. I even had two staff.' She glanced up, watching another fruit bat wing overhead. 'As you said, one never knows what lies around life's corners. After my parents died, I returned to run this guest house.'

With a second awamori in hand, Suzuki felt the same warm, floating sensation she'd shared with Teizo in the Kobe bar several days earlier. She soon found herself talking shop. Aragaki was, after all, in the same line of business. She related humorous stories of life behind the reception desk of a big city hotel. At these, Aragaki laughed, listening intently.

Suddenly, a shrill scream interrupted them, piercing the night.

Suzuki leapt up and glanced about. 'Aya!'

She hurried to the entranceway, and without slipping on her sandals, rushed barefooted along the darkened path.

'Aya!

At the end of the pathway, she stopped dead. A laneway lamp illuminated her daughter like a stage light. A snake lay coiled in front of her small sandaled foot. It wasn't moving, but the wavering head said it was about to.

Aragaki strode quietly forward, and her voice was firm and calm. 'Aya, he only wants to get away. Step back slowly … that's it. Slowly. Back … back. Well done.'

The child edged away from the light, turned, and rushed into her mother's arms. Sensing the threat had passed, the serpent slithered off, vanishing into a coral rock wall.

Suzuki lifted her daughter, gripping her firmly. 'Was that poisonous?'

'Yes. Very,' said Aragaki. 'It's a *habu*. They're active in spring, looking for mates.' She rubbed the girl's back. 'It's perfectly safe in the daytime, little one. Just wear shoes if you're going out at night and make lots of noise when you're walking. The snakes will sense you coming and escape on their own.'

Suzuki glanced down at her own bare feet. 'I don't think we'll be going anywhere at night—or tomorrow night,' she said. As they walked back to the guesthouse, she asked, 'Do you have any children?'

'No.'

'They certainly keep you sharp. Phew! I could do with another drink.'

First things were first, however; she helped her mother and daughter to the bath, laid out their pyjamas and fluffed their futons. Once settled, she returned to the deck for a nightcap.

The night sky shimmered with more stars than could be believed. Crickets chirped, beetles purred through the air, and jets strobed their way south. Far above them, a satellite skimmed the stardust, a pinprick of light whose destination, unlike the jet passengers, would never be achieved.

The tide had quietened. Its gentle sloughing at the foot of the garden said it was about to turn.

Suzuki sipped her drink, glancing now and again at the kitchen where Aragaki moved about, washing, drying and arranging dishes, preparing for the following day's fare. Something about this hard-working, seemingly independent woman who valued family, yet had no children of her own, intrigued her. Where had her husband fitted into this picture? Aragaki had only mentioned him in passing and said nothing of his death. The light in the room above the deck was still on.

Suzuki finished her drink. To worry about anything after three glasses of awamori seemed impossible. The world at that very moment felt just right.

* * *

The next morning, the clam-hunting party assembled on the deck after breakfast, awaiting their instructions.

'First,' said Aragaki, 'we check the tide tables. Four hours on either side of low tide is fine, but the lower the better.' She handed Suzuki and her mother each a plastic bucket and a hand hoe. Having donned sunhats and sandals, they trooped through the garden gate below the deck and descended the path. They moved slowly, timidly, through the tropical foliage until their feet touched the wet sand of the estuary. Aragaki led them out on to the flats where the mud oozed and squirted like chocolate mousse beneath their sandals. The channel lay ahead, the sandbar beyond it.

'Is the channel deep?' Suzuki asked, trying not to step on the holes of burrowing creatures.

'You can wade across at the lowest point of the tide.' Aragaki regarded her for a moment. 'You seem set on that sandbar, don't you?'

Suzuki laughed. 'A sugar white island in a bay of blue—looks like a small paradise.'

'It certainly does. But it can be a dangerous place when the tide turns.' She halted. To the clam hunters, she said, 'Let's begin here, shall we? First, look for little holes in the mud. See, like these ones.'

Suzuki, her mother, and daughter formed a scrum around the tiny openings in the sand.

'There's probably a steamer—a soft-shell clam—lurking beneath. Let's take a look, shall we?' Aragaki stamped the mud. Something squirted. Aya squealed. 'There!' she cried.

Sure enough, as Aragaki raked with her hoe, clams revealed themselves. 'Where there are a few, there'll be more. Make a hole, then sift the mud with your fingers, like this.' Soon there were a dozen molluscs in the bucket. 'The small ones are the most tender—that's what you ate in your miso soup last night.'

As the sun crept higher, their buckets grew heavier. At last, Aragaki said, 'I think that will do us for today. We want to leave some for next time, don't we?'

The adventure kept Aya chattering excitedly all the way back across the mud flats. From the other side of the estuary came the sound of a hammer on steel. Shielding her eyes against the glare, Suzuki discerned a small boat in the distance that sat awkwardly balanced on top of oil drums. She hadn't noticed it earlier. Now she saw that there were two men working above and below the boat: the one scraping the hull was short and stocky with wild hair and dark skin; the other, who hovered over the engine with a hammer in his hand, was slim and wore a straw hat.

'Who are they?' she asked.

Aragaki followed Suzuki's gaze. 'Ohayo!'

The men acknowledged her with a wave.

'Friends?' said Suzuki.

'My cousin's sons. Looks like cleaning day. They use the tide to put their boat up and work on it when it goes out.' She grinned. 'That's Kabira cleverness.'

When they returned to the house, Aya volunteered to help her rinse the clams in the kitchen and put them aside for dinner, while Suzuki and her mother rested.

A short while later, her daughter came running with tears in her eyes. 'My shells are gone. Someone's stolen my shells!'

Sure enough, when they stepped to the guesthouse entrance, half of the shells they had collected the day before were missing.

There was one odd thing that Suzuki observed: a series of small trails in the sand led away from the crime scene and disappeared into the garden. She peered cautiously through the foliage.

Alerted by the girl's whimpering, Aragaki joined them. 'Oh no—did they take your shells?'

'Who's *they*?' Suzuki asked.

Aragaki parted the branches of a hibiscus bush and led them into the cool depths of the garden. After a few paces, she bent down and lifted a shard of broken earthen jar. 'Look. Can you see your shells?'

They peered downwards and the sniffing child said, 'Yes! That one, the white one with the blue spots! How did it get there?'

The shells were bunched together, huddle-like. Aragaki picked up the largest and pointed at a tiny pincer guarding its mouth opening. 'This little guy took your shell as his new house. It's a hermit crab. As they grow bigger, they have to find a bigger home. Seems like your shell was the perfect fit.'

The young girl held the shell with a look of fascination.

'You've given him a new house,' Aragaki said.

'*Yadokari*—Hermit Crab Guesthouse.' Suzuki laughed. 'I guess we all need a roof over our head, don't we?'

* * *

The clock was ticking.

Suzuki decided to take stock of what she'd gleaned so far, weigh the value of the information, and decide her next move. It was time to play tourist.

They took a picnic lunch of rice balls and cold jasmine-oolong tea which Aragaki had prepared for them, and with their swimwear pinching uncomfortably at their pale city skin, set off by car for Yonehara Beach.

A short distance along the coast, beyond the other half of Kabira township, they pulled into a parking area with a kiosk and toilet block. On the other side of a line of casuarina trees lay a beach and a lagoon where clumps of coral stood dripping above the receding tide. Further out, past the reef and its pulverizing waves, the East China Sea stretched forever.

They erected the parasol Aragaki had lent them and wasted no time venturing into the turquoise water. Though Golden Week was still several weeks away, the beach was lively with young families and couples; their loud voices and Kansai accents marked them as holidaying mainlanders.

She watched her mother and daughter wallowing in the shallows, carefree and happy, and wondered how she'd made it this far. Moreover, she wondered what she was even doing here. She surveyed the lagoon; a hot, dry breeze had lifted, ruffling the casuarina trees, but the water remained calm and waves no longer thundered across the reef. The tide was on its way in.

It gave her an idea.

Beneath the parasol, she took out her phone and called the one person who knew more about the sea than she could learn in a lifetime.

'Any perils in paradise?' he answered.

'Plenty—but we'll survive. How's the weather in Kobe?'

'Perfect for fishing.'

'A question for you. How does one find out the tide movements for Kabira on 28 March last year?'

There was a moment of silence, and Suzuki could almost hear him thinking. She suspected he liked such queries because they cast him back to his previous life as a submariner.

'If I said that I have no idea, would you be angry?'

'Yes.'

'I'll call you back in ten minutes. That is—if you're not too busy.'

She gazed at the sunbathers, the shimmering water, at her mother and daughter playing joyfully in the wavelets. 'Not too busy,' she said.

She thanked him and hung up, reminding herself to pick him up a bottle of Omoto awamori before their return.

Two hungry people soon emerged from the lagoon and advanced on her. They dined on their rice balls and tea, and when finished, Suzuki asked her mother and daughter to go for ice cream at the kiosk.

Her phone vibrated. 'That was quick,' she said.

'The Kuroshima Research Station operates tide gauges for Ishigaki and the surrounding islands. They said they can send me low and high tide times for 28 March.'

'How do you do this?'

'Life is simple—just add seawater.'

* * *

Returning along the coastal highway, with mother and daughter dozing and the warm, heavy air vague with the smell of vanilla ice cream, Suzuki fought drowsiness. All at once, a flash of vivid colour caught her eye among the roadside banyan trees. A huge and brightly painted *shiisa*—the lion-dog that Okinawans mount on their gate walls and rooftops to ward off evil spirits—stood guard outside a large white tin shed. A sign outside announced, 'Atelier Shiisa'. Funny, she couldn't recall seeing it earlier that morning.

Pulling into the shade of a large tree, she left her mother and daughter asleep, and ventured inside. Table after table lay covered with cheerfully painted shiisa. Three staff sat at the far end of the shed, dexterously painting clay figurines, so that no two lion-dogs were alike in colour.

The prices were a little steep, but art was like that, so she settled on a medium-sized shiisa painted blue and yellow with big eyes and comically large white teeth. The colours reminded her of an Omoto awamori bottle label.

'Just passing through?' enquired the staff, carefully wrapping her purchase and placing it in a carry box. She looked in her forties and wore a bright red bandanna about her long dark hair.

'We're staying in Kabira.'

'Taken a glass bottom boat yet?'

'Maybe tomorrow.'

'My husband says viewing conditions are perfect. He's a boat captain.' She paused. 'Where are you staying?'

'At Yadokari Guesthouse.'

'Wonderful! The owner's my sister-in-law.'

'Your husband is the owner's brother?'

'Kazuha Aragaki? Yes. Tell her that Mizuho said hello.'

Suzuki thanked her and returned to the car where her mother and daughter remained asleep, their faces red and gleaming in the heat. Back on the highway, her thoughts turned to Aragaki and the uncanny fact that she was surrounded by family—sister, brother, cousins….

Her phone vibrated.

She slowed the car and pulled over. The screenshot of the tide table for 28 March the previous year had arrived. She'd have to buy him *two* bottles of awamori!

Back in Kabira, as she turned into the laneway leading down to the guesthouse, she noticed a vehicle parked outside the mini market on the corner. It was the same small truck whose driver had sold them mango smoothies on the coastal highway the day before.

Passing the playground, she sighted the young girl. She brought the car to a stop and called a greeting through the window.

The girl grinned, flashing her gap-tooth.

'So, you finished all your homework?' Suzuki asked.

'Yes,' she said proudly, slowing her swing.

'Thank you for telling me about swimming yesterday. We've just been to Yonehara. What a wonderful place.'

The girl nodded. 'We go there on weekends.'

Suzuki left the car running, got out and walked over. Down in the channel, the sandbar gleamed brightly.

'Remember you told me that you'd seen people swimming down there?'

The girl nodded.

'Can you tell me exactly what you saw?'

* * *

After cleansing their bodies of salt and sand, the three women descended to the dining room, and in the same crowded atmosphere of delicious aromas of the previous night, enjoyed another sumptuous dinner of local Okinawan cuisine.

While her mother and daughter chatted spiritedly between mouthfuls, Suzuki chewed her food slowly and with less joy. Exhaustion consumed her; the same feeling that came each time when facts had been unearthed and left to ferment. Only one ingredient now remained unaccounted for—the final catalyst that would bring the essence to the surface. Without an outright confession from Kazuha Aragaki, the way in which Kenjiro Miki had died on his birthday would remain as stated in the coroner's official records. She reminded herself that she was not here to seek a confession, but to determine if there were grounds for a case of criminal negligence, possibly murder, to be brought against his wife.

'Your clams are served!' Aragaki said, placing bowls of miso soup beside them. 'Enjoy.'

Suzuki's phone rang. She pulled it from her pocket, dismayed to find Chiaki Yamamoto calling. She turned the device to vibrate mode and slipped it back into her pocket.

The sun had almost set when they finished their dinner. Not wanting to miss another western sky aflame, Suzuki and her mother retired to the deck, leaving her daughter at the dining table to draw pictures on pieces of scrap paper.

Another long day had passed, and Suzuki refrained from drinking any alcohol, knowing that she would soon have to take a walk in order to speak with Chiaki Yamamoto in private.

Key information had come to light, yet she was not ready to divulge the details; rather, she had questions.

She stifled a yawn. Glancing through the dining room door, she noticed that Aragaki had paused from clearing the table to chat with her daughter.

All at once, the woman's expression changed. She reached down and picked up the child's picture and a deep frown creased her forehead.

Suzuki sat up. She sensed something amiss. 'Would you mind taking Aya to bed now, please?' she asked her mother quickly.

'But it's only eight-thirty.'

'Please—just do it!'

Her mother gave a start but rose from her seat and made her way to the dining room just as Aragaki stepped on to the deck.

Suzuki was standing now, her senses on high alert.

'Where did you get this?' Aragaki said, holding up the piece of paper. Her tone was as taut as a piano wire.

Suzuki glimpsed squiggles of a beach, people with lumpy heads and smiling faces, a big sun … her phone vibrated again.

Aragaki turned over the paper.

Suzuki froze—the coroner's report.

'You came here to spy on me?'

'Please let me explain—'

'Who are you?'

'Please….' Suzuki felt her muscles deaden and something like a mild electric current sizzle across her skin.

'Who sent you?'

She opened her mouth but her lips had turned to wood.

'Who sent you!' Aragaki's eyes shone fiercely.

'Chiaki Yamamoto.' Again, her phone vibrated.

Aragaki's jaw quivered, her voice now a fearsome growl. 'I want you and your family to leave this guesthouse. Immediately.'

Air caught in Suzuki's throat. She felt as if she was drowning.

'Now!' screamed Aragaki.

* * *

The highway lay dark and empty ahead of them.

As the small car climbed the hillside leading out of Kabira, her mother sobbed. Her daughter, oblivious to the flurry of movement and noise that had transpired earlier, lay fast asleep in the back seat.

It was now a little before 10 p.m., and Suzuki had calmed herself enough to focus on driving them safely back to Ishigaki township where she would have to find a hotel with a vacancy. A tremor came and went through her right hand. It hadn't been there before.

Descending on to the coast, a flashing blue light caught her eye in the rear vision mirror. It advanced on them at speed.

Moments later, the sound of a loudspeaker split the night air and the words which followed filled Suzuki with doom.

'What's going on?' her mother sniffled.

'Just wait. Let me deal with this.'

At a hard shoulder near the seashore, she slowed, then brought the car to a stop. She listened to the crunch of gravel beneath boots and glimpsed a flashlight ranging ahead of them.

'Ms Mami Suzuki?'

The officer leaned down to the window. He was young and spoke with politeness.

'Yes?'

He peered inside, at the mother first, then at the sleeping child engulfed by hurriedly packed clothing. 'My aunt would like you to return to the guesthouse,' he said. 'She apologizes for her behaviour and for your inconvenience. She would like to talk. Will you follow me back to Kabira?'

'Your aunt? You mean Kazuha Aragaki?'

'Will you follow me?'

In the business of private investigation there were rare moments when an unseen, divine hand suddenly presses the 'pause' button on reality. This was one of those moments.

Suzuki glanced at her mother, tired and red-eyed, incapable of any further mental or physical action. She looked back at her daughter, blissfully asleep in the back seat. In the rear vision mirror she caught a glimpse of herself, exhausted—emotionally and physically washed up. What the mirror did not show was the shame and regret she felt for involving her family in her work. It was a disastrous decision.

'We'll follow you,' she said.

Few words were spoken as Aragaki and her police officer nephew helped to resettle Suzuki's mother and daughter in their upstairs room. But after Aragaki had directed her nephew to the kitchen, telling him to help himself to the food and beer, she joined Suzuki on the deck, placing a tray with glasses, ice, water, and a fresh bottle of awamori on the table between them.

'I don't usually drink, but tonight I think we could both do with some fortifying. Will you join me?' she said.

Suzuki said nothing. She watched Aragaki proceed to mix the drinks and then hand her a glass. They sat facing the bay, their backs to the lamplight, their faces obscured in shadow. There was no 'Kanpai'; they drank without speaking.

'So,' Aragaki said, at last. 'How does this go? You tell me, then I tell you?'

Through the dining room window, Suzuki glimpsed the nephew sipping his beer and tucking into his late-night supper, hardly giving the two women outside a glance.

'You sent him to catch us?' Suzuki asked.

'He's a good boy. My brother's son.'

'Your brother—the boat captain?'

'Like I said, Kabira is one big family.'

The tide had receded and up from the rock pools came strange popping and hissing noises, which mingled with the splashing sounds of larger aquatic life out in the channel. Somewhere far off, thunder sounded.

'Chiaki Yamamoto never did like me,' Aragaki said. 'She thought I was too simple, too rural, the girl from way down south where the mangoes grow. When I found out I couldn't have children, it confirmed her belief that I was useless. So, when Kenjiro died, there could be only one person to blame for his passing.' She took a sip of her drink and laughed dryly. 'Well then? Now that I have shown you how to dig for clams, perhaps you'll tell me how you dig dirt.'

For the second time in as many days, Suzuki wondered how she'd come to be here, on this warm March evening, on this deck overlooking a serene bay, in this sleepy town on this tiny island at the very bottom of Japan.

The time was ripe. It was now or never.

'Your husband, Kenjiro Miki, was an alcoholic. As a birthday present last year, on 28 March, you took him out to the sandbar at low tide with a cooler box of drinks and two chairs. You stayed for one or two with him, then you left, knowing that he would likely continue drinking and be unable to get back to shore because of the strong tidal current flowing into the bay.'

Aragaki said nothing, her face unreadable in the shadows.

Suzuki continued: 'I'm assuming no one would have heard your husband's cries for help because the boat tours had finished, and after this guesthouse there is only mangrove forest. I say *heard*, not seen, because there is a schoolgirl who lives up the road. She had something interesting to say.' Suzuki paused, but Aragaki maintained her silence.

'After school, the girl does her homework, then she visits the playground. The playground has a clear view of the channel and the sandbar at low tide. Although she can't remember the exact date, the girl said it was about this time last year that she saw two people wade out to the sandbar. No one ever goes out on the sandbar, at least not local people. The strange thing was, she said, these two people *appeared* to be having a picnic.

'On the day your husband drowned, low tide occurred at 3.35 p.m. according to the Kuroshima Research Centre here on Ishigaki Island. You would have known this because you collect clams. Three-thirty is also when the girl gets home from school. It takes her fifteen to twenty minutes to finish her homework, therefore, she would have arrived at the playground before 4 p.m. That's when she first saw the two people on the sandbar. Later, one of them leaves, taking a chair, and crosses the channel back to the shore.

'In the police report, Kenjiro Yamamato's body was found by a pearl farm employee around 6.30 p.m. The coroner puts the time of drowning at sometime between 4 p.m. and 6 p.m. when the in-coming current was at its strongest. You no doubt already know that it takes roughly six hours for a tide to run from low to high.'

'When I asked the girl if she had told anyone else this information, she said 'no'. When I asked her why, she said because no one had asked her. She never saw what happened to the other person on the sandbar because she returned to her apartment just after 5 p.m., when the community public address system tells the local kids it's home time. Your husband, therefore, must have drowned between 5 p.m and 6 p.m. in a current that was strong enough to carry his body across the bay to the pearl farm.'

Aragaki raised her glass to her lips. She drank it dry. 'You're right,' she said without emotion. 'He was an alcoholic. He was an alcoholic even before he came here.'

'I'm not here to pass judgement,' said Suzuki. 'My job was only to gather information.'

'I wouldn't have picked you for a private investigator. You seem too nice. I thought your type only spied on cheating husbands and wives … you don't work at a hotel then, do you?'

'This is my side job.'

Aragaki glanced quickly at her. 'You must need the money.'

'Believe me, I do.'

'Divorced?

'Yes.'

'I won't say I envy you, but there was a time when I would have. Getting married was the biggest mistake of my life.'

The sound of thunder grew nearer. Suzuki glanced towards the dining room; the nephew was still seated at the table, all-consumed in his wonderful meal, as if he had forgotten about events of the past hour, or even that his aunt and her houseguest were outside talking.

Suzuki felt a strange wave of relief. How bizarre that she had revealed everything she knew, not to her client, but to the very subject of her investigation. Why had she done that?

Was it because Aragaki had shown remorse—even compassion? The very same woman who, to which all information so far pointed, had aided in some way her husband's drowning?

It was Aragaki's turn to speak.

'You said that we never know what lies around life's corners. Before my parents died, my life in Tokyo was pure misery. It sounds strange but when they died, suddenly it was, in an odd way, a good thing. It gave me a fresh chance at life, a chance to escape Tokyo and return here, to the place where I grew up. My brother and sister encouraged me to take over the guesthouse business. And so I agreed.

'But there was the problem of Kenjiro—and his drinking. In his last years at the company, he had been making things difficult at my restaurant, always bringing his junior colleagues and associates to eat and drink, and not charging them even though they insisted on paying. I worked hard to build up my business, I had part-time staff and suppliers to pay … I felt like I was running on the spot.

'Eventually, I sold the business to a friend and returned to Kabira, knowing that Kenjiro would have to follow after his retirement in a year's time. He couldn't look after himself—he couldn't even cook—so he hired a housekeeper for his final year in Tokyo. I thought life here would be easier, and it was for that first year. Business was good. Relatives helped me. I was busy. I was happy. Then, when Kenjiro arrived, everything changed. I encouraged him to take up fishing and join the golf club in Ishigaki to keep busy while I ran the guesthouse. Instead, he sat around feeling sorry for himself, criticizing the locals and their ways, always talking about how great Tokyo is, and always drinking.

'He even began to bother the guests. He would drink, fall asleep on this deck, then wake and pester them. Sometimes he would fall down and the guests would call me, worried and concerned. But it was just his way of getting attention. It grew worse. Sometimes, he stole the female guests' underwear, and once, walked into the women's bathroom naked. The Internet reviews were devastating. Soul-destroying! Guesthouses with creepy old drunks get only one star.'

From across the bay came a sound like an audience clapping, a pitter-pattering that grew louder. Aragaki finished her glass. 'Another?'

'Thank you,' said Suzuki. She watched the woman refill the glasses with ice and pour generously, stirring in the water. 'That's why you renamed it?'

'Minshuku Shiokaze—the Seabreeze Inn—is a little old-fashioned, don't you think?' She handed Suzuki her drink. 'I wanted young people from Kansai and Kanto to come, so I called it Yadokari Guesthouse.'

'And they did?'

'Slowly. Little by little, after a year we are busy again.' She turned to Suzuki. 'You could say I've turned one of life's corners.'

What *could* Suzuki say? It was a story often told; one which rang true of husbands burdening their wives on retirement. It wasn't fair that a man who had given forty years of his life to company and family should be scorned by his wife in retirement, but it also wasn't fair that a husband should expect three meals a day and someone to clean-up after him while he sat around drinking and doing sweet nothing. She wasn't sure that that had been the situation between Aragaki and her husband, but it was a generally accepted reality. Suzuki personally knew the elderly men who dressed in dapper suits and arrived with business satchels each morning to the Orient Hotel's first-floor cafe. She also knew that most of them were pretending—they were retired. They came to chat, drink coffee, and read the paper with their fellow 'actors'. One had even confided in her that his wife didn't even know he was retired, and that it was best that way because he feared being cast on the heap if she ever found out.

Not all realities were the same—not all husbands were burdens and not all wives scornful. But this was a hard-working woman who had wrested control of her life from an alcoholic husband. 'Did your husband want to die?' Suzuki asked.

'If he did, it wasn't because of me.'

'Did you try professional help?'

'You mean, like an AA group?'

'Counselling.'

'He was too stubborn … too ashamed.'

A breeze lifted. The pitter-pattering was now a fearful drumming noise, growing louder as it crossed the bay.

'Rain,' said Aragaki.

'We should go inside.'

Aragaki took another sip. 'I think I'll sit here a while.'

Suzuki smelt the earthy sweetness of the breeze and felt the rain thundering towards her. But the awamori had dulled her nerves, slowed her reactions, and she felt as if her body had made up its own mind.

'So, what happens now?' Aragaki asked.

Before Suzuki could answer, a droplet splattered on the wooden deck. Then another, and another, until a deluge was upon them. Raindrops that could have filled a shot glass careened down, pelting the papaya tree leaves to deafening effect. When Suzuki glanced at Aragaki, she saw that her face was held upwards to the rain, her eyes closed.

Aragaki's nephew, peering out the dining room entranceway, called, 'Is everyone okay?'

Aragaki put her hand on Suzuki's arm. Over the roar, she heard her say, 'Come with me. There's something I want to show you.'

They towelled off inside, and to her bemused nephew, Aragaki said, 'Mango ice cream. Help yourself.' She went to the fridge and retrieved it for him, and at the same moment, slipped into her pocket something which Suzuki could not see.

They took umbrellas and made their way along the path where fallen leaves and flowers leapt about animated as the rain hurled down. Aragaki led the way through the small orchard, and although she could not tell what kind, Suzuki could smell the pungency of fallen fruit. They reached the traditional Okinawan house, the place where Aragaki had grown up.

Stepping across the threshold, she motioned Suzuki inside. They shook the water from their bodies and smoothed back their hair. Aragaki flicked a switch and a bulb set the rustic interior aglow. The wooden floor was smooth underfoot, the house neither eerie nor comfortable. It reminded Suzuki of her grandmother's house on the mountainside in Himeji.

Halfway along the hallway, Aragaki slid back a paper door and turned on a light. To Suzuki's eyes it was a traditional Japanese room with worn tatami mats and a sacred *tokonoma* space in the corner. Portrait photos hung on the walls and she didn't need to be told that these were Aragaki's ancestors. Crossing the room, her host gently opened a set of ornate doors and touched a switch. The Buddhist family altar glowed, crowded with brass ornaments and lined with gold leaf. Miniature banners stood on a shelf inside, each bearing an ancestor's name, and beside these, dishes of oranges and rice had been placed as offerings.

Aragaki laid two cushions before the altar. With Suzuki at her side, she lit a candle and a stick of incense, then rang the bell. Placing her hands together, she bowed her head.

Suzuki noted the newest addition to the line of small banners.

Its kanji characters read:

靴汁院英担酸押信士

And although she could not read this *kaimyo*, the posthumous Buddhist name, she instinctively knew who it belonged to. She glanced up at his portrait; a large-faced man with meaty jowls and thinning grey hair looking back down on her. There was nothing sad or solemn in his expression. He looked content even, as if he had lived a full life and no one could ever take it away from him. No one—except himself.

'I've never done this before,' Aragaki said, and took from her pocket the item Suzuki had been unable to see in the kitchen. It was a small can of beer. 'I did not think it appropriate. But after our talk, I realized this is probably what he wants most right now.'

She opened the can and placed it in front of his banner. 'His ashes aren't here—they're with his family—but I believe this is where his spirit resides. With me.'

Turning to Suzuki, she said, 'I know what you want to ask me. So, I will tell you this, I believe Kenjiro died the day he retired. He pleaded with the company's board of directors to keep him on as an advisor, but they said that they had to make room for new talent and that their decision was final. He was at a loss from the moment arrived here—and his drinking only made it worse. In the end, I believe he'd had enough. All he wanted was to drift away peacefully.'

* * *

The mood on Peach Air flight MM330 was calm and quiet. Passengers, perhaps contemplating their adventures, wore the expressions of satisfied tourists returning home to tell stories and disperse souvenirs.

With her daughter and mother sharing bags of dried mango and Ishigaki rock sugar, Suzuki eased her head back on the seat rest. She looked out at the endless plane of blue, which stretched beneath the clouds. She felt glad to be leaving. It had been less a working-holiday than actual work itself. She was exhausted.

Still, she could not shut down her thoughts. Nothing was ever as it seemed; not even her sense of right and wrong felt trustworthy anymore. Professional obligation had pitted itself against her integrity as a woman, for whom triumph over adversity was akin to survival. She had to press on, through this hall of mirrors, hoping an answer would present itself. It might not be the perfect answer, but it had to be the best one.

Presently, the captain made his announcement, and the plane began its descent into Kansai Airport. The hard lines of the Osaka seaboard crept into view with its crowded container ports and man-made islands, forested with distillation towers and gas refineries, so different to the lush lumpiness of Ishigaki Island. The plane touched down, and upon disembarking, the grandmother took granddaughter for a meal at McDonalds, allowing Suzuki to retreat to a quiet corner and make a phone call.

Chiaki Yamamoto sounded pleased—buoyant even.

Suzuki began, 'I intend to give you a full written report detailing my investigation into the possible involvement of your brother's wife in his drowning death last year. However, I would like to give you a summary of my findings now if that is convenient?'

'Please do.'

'Having conducted a thorough investigation of the location of your brother's death and spending time at his wife's guesthouse, I must be frank—I am unable to say with confidence that his wife contributed to his death. In fact, my research has found that there have been three previous drownings in the same area over the past ten years—each one of the deceased was a visitor to the island.'

Chiaki Yamamoto said nothing.

Suzuki continued: 'During my stay at your sister-in-law's guesthouse, she talked about her family, in a conversational sense, and invited me into her childhood home where she tends her family *butsudan*. In my opinion, she appears to be a woman with a strong spiritual connection to her family members, her parents, and your brother Kenjiro included, and as such, pays her respects regularly.'

Chiaki Yamamoto's silence lengthened.

When she finally spoke, it was not in the dark and disappointed tone that Suzuki had had expected.

'Thank you for your summary, Ms Suzuki. I'm greatly impressed with your professionalism, and I look forward to reading your findings in detail. Perhaps this is a coincidence, but on visiting my uranaishi this morning, something very interesting has come to light.'

'Oh?' said Suzuki, frowning.

'They said that my brother's spirit had found peace. Something has occurred which they were unable to explain, suffice to say, that he is no longer restless. He is content.'

Suzuki did not know what to say.

'Rest assured,' Chiaki Yamamoto continued, 'our agreed-upon fee will be paid regardless of this outcome, along with your expenses of course. Please send me the report and your receipts at your earliest convenience. Thank you once again for all you have done.'

* * *

They met at Bar Ember Days the following Friday night. She was running late, on account of a tour group that had rescheduled its Golden Week bookings, and he, as usual, was early. He wore black jeans and sneakers, a white polo shirt under his leather jacket, casual yet sartorial—in what she'd have called 'old rock 'n' roll' style. Spring nights still carried a light chill, and as such, she wore a tan trench coat over her beige UNIQLO dress pants and a Spanish lace blouse, revealing just enough of her forearms to suggest time in the tropics.

It was early evening. With no live jazz billed, the sofas and tables were occupied by office workers from the financial district, enjoying quiet end-of-week drinks. Teizo wore the face of a man looking forward to something, but pretending not to. She found it cute.

'I've made it worth your wait,' she said, sliding on to the bar stool beside him. 'This is for you.' She presented him with a colourful carry bag.

He pulled out the two bottles inside. 'Omoto awamori?' he said.

'So?'

'Thank you.'

'No, thank *you*. Your help never goes unappreciated.'

She felt like gin—something refreshing but not too sweet. He suggested gin rickeys. They ordered, and when the drinks arrived, toasted the end of the working week.

'Do spirits get thirsty?' she asked him. 'I mean, the deceased and the departed kind.'

'That's an odd question.'

'It's just that when a woman makes an offering of beer to her husband's spirit, all suspicion of her hand in his death suddenly disappears.'

She had seen the look on Teizo's face before. It was curiosity. He was waiting for more.

To the rattling noise of a cocktail shaker and the brassy notes of Chet Baker's trumpet, she began to unpack the case. It had, like most cases, started with intrigue but then spiralled into an adventure, which had left her bewildered, confused, and questioning her own worth as a private investigator. It took a second gin rickey to conclude with the mysterious question of why Chiaki Yamamoto had had a change of heart. Suzuki touched Teizo's arm and said sympathetically, 'You know, I feel as exhausted as you look.'

'And I'm only listening.'

'Thank you.'

'Maybe the uranaishi picked up on something your client told her. Something that might not be good for their business.'

'What do you mean?'

'Well … if your client had mentioned to the uranaishi that she'd hired a private investigator, there might be potential for a formal inquiry into her brother's death. It might have unnerved them. You see, uranaishi are like mushrooms—they prefer quiet, shady places.'

'Hmm, I hadn't thought about it like that.'

'What mystifies me is this. On her brother's birthday, the incoming tide just happened to coincide with dinner service at the guesthouse, meaning that Aragaki had a perfectly good reason to leave her husband alone on the sandbar. He must have been thirsty.'

'Which brings me back to my first question—do spirits get thirsty?'

Teizo picked up his glass and drained it dry. 'All I can say is that when I'm dead and gone, I won't pester you for a drink.'

In the dimness of the bar, with a trumpet soloing and glasses clinking, her hand found his and pressed it firmly.

'I know you will,' she said.

Isle of Cats

Summer had arrived and the city simmered.

Having drifted up from the Philippines and delivered their rain throughout June and July, the warm air currents of the *Kuroshio*, the Black Stream, now ground to a standstill over Kobe. Nights were the worst when the pent-up heat of the day oozed from the concrete and the undulating hum of air conditioners played background to the dreams of the lucky few who slept. Those who couldn't, went to bed grumpy and awoke grumpier. Only Suzuki's mother's hydrangeas of pastel pink and blue nodded happily in the humid sea breeze.

With holiday season approaching and the hotel growing busier, the heat had begun to exact its toll. Suzuki watched sympathetically as guests left the lobby spritely and cheerful in their crisp collars, only to return red-faced and depleted with clothes clinging to their bodies like wet tissue paper.

Adding to her own discomfort was the new reception manager, Goto. Since the start of the rainy season, his administrative meddling had sent ripples of frustration throughout the front desk staff, giving ever more credence to the rumour that he'd gotten his post through family connections instead of professional merit.

Brooding over her tea in the cafeteria one sultry afternoon, Suzuki looked up to find a junior staff member standing before her.

'Ms Suzuki?' said the young woman. 'I'm Miku Shibata ... from the accounts section. Sorry to bother you during your tea break. May I speak with you for a moment?'

'Sure.'

The young woman seated herself opposite. 'I'm an acquaintance of Chiaki Yamamoto sensei.'

'Oh?' Suzuki's senses prickled. Her gaze ran quickly over the young woman; her pale complexion, high cheekbones, perfect teeth, impeccable makeup and pink high-gloss nails. 'She's an interesting person.'

'Yamamoto sensei was my *sado* teacher at university. Last week we happened to meet, and she mentioned you might be able to help me....'

Suzuki waited.

'Not *me* personally ... my sister,' Shibata said. 'She lives here in Kobe, near Sannomiya.'

Alarm bells clanged inside Suzuki's head. She glanced about the cafeteria, busy with tea-breaking staff, then back at Shibata. Leaning forward, she said, 'Best we talk outside.'

'Yes, yes ... of course.'

'Do you take the train?'

Shibata nodded.

'I'm off at five. Let's walk to the station, shall we?'

They exchanged phone numbers, rose from the table and parted as if it was the summer bargain sales they had been discussing.

* * *

By late afternoon the sea breeze had died, and not even the passing Coast Guard launches could ruffle the oily sheen of the harbour. Dabbing her brow with a handkerchief, Suzuki stepped from the hotel staff entrance and crossed to the esplanade. Miku Shibata stood beside a mooring bollard, a phone pressed to her ear. On sighting Suzuki, she waved.

As they fell into stride, Suzuki let the younger woman do the talking.

'Yamamoto sensei is a second mother to me. We speak frankly on all matters. When we last met, I mentioned that my sister and her husband have a family problem ... and she recommended your services to me.'

Suzuki, her face and neck glistening, waited for more.

'The matter is deeply personal, and my sister would prefer to discuss it in person,' Shibata continued. 'I spoke with her just a few moments ago. Would you be willing to meet tomorrow?'

'In Sannomiya?'

'At Cafe Freundlieb.'

'The old church cafe?'

'Is six-thirty convenient?'

It was Teizo's birthday the next day and she had made dinner arrangements for them on Kitanozaka Street for 7.30 p.m. Cafe Freundlieb was a five-minute walk up the hill.

'What does your sister look like?'

'I'll send you a photo tonight.'

When they reached the end of the esplanade and crossed to the train station entrance, Suzuki took Shibata aside. 'To be absolutely clear, what I do outside the hotel is entirely my business. This meeting cannot be discussed with anyone else.'

Shibata's eyes widened. 'I understand completely—thank you so much for meeting with me.'

The two women then parted for different platforms.

* * *

Private investigation was a lot like boarding a rush-hour *kaisoku* train. There was an art involved. One had to push, but not be too pushy. One had to find a way inside while avoiding close contact. Squeezing into a space beside the door, Suzuki watched those with lesser mettle give up, or be forced back on to the platform to await the next train. It was a metaphor for modern-day survival: fighting for your place without stepping on the toes of others.

As the train pulled away, the wilting faces of other working women passed by in a pale blur. The scene caused her to wonder: How many women worked in the hotel industry? How many were in private investigating? How many did both? It was an unlikely pairing—providing comfort to travellers by day and delving into peoples' lives by night.

To be sure, both professions required canny communication skills and an ability to interpret and anticipate the needs of Kobe's social strata. But that's where the likenesses ended. To be a private eye was to bear witness to misery and suffering, to know the dark sides of peoples' lives, and for the most part, to not be able to do anything about it. Hunting a pearl thief was not the same as searching for a house guest's lost passport; nor was chasing a runaway sushi chef along a remote coastline the same as searching for a lost child in a hotel lobby. Private investigating was an unpredictable and unknowable business. No wonder the banks would never lend money to anyone in such a profession. That's why the day job mattered; it was safe, secure, and busy. The greatest unsolved mystery to date was how she managed to do both.

Later that evening, as she reclined in her old massage chair, she received an image from Miku Shibata. Ami Koba was a starkly different version of her younger sister; full-faced, cropped-haired, no fan of make-up, and a gaze that was all business. Suzuki wondered what her profession might be.

* * *

The next day, after confirming the restaurant reservation, she swapped her tight-fitting hotel uniform for a linen one-piece in muted lime green and a pair of turquoise leather pumps. Her handbag held her business documents, a tea bottle, and a small gift for Teizo.

Outside Sannomiya Station, the evening hummed with promise. The after-five crowds of bar and restaurant-goers had begun their tidal flow into the entertainment districts. July heat be damned, the city would not sleep again tonight.

Suzuki made her way up Flower Road, but after five minutes she was sweating profusely, and her ankles swelled painfully.

Cafe Freundlieb was a popular fixture on the Kobe cafe scene and it stood impressively, if not conspicuously, on a back street lined with modern office buildings and apartments. Porches and Jaguars crowded its car park, and through its Gothic-arched entranceway, a mostly well-heeled female clientele came and went.

Inside, Suzuki passed by the bakery with its hovering cake-buyers and ascended the old church's wooden stairway until the sounds of clinking coffee cups and murmured conversations materialized into a vast hall. Across its black and white checked floor, tables with bentwood chairs held huddles of iced-coffee drinkers and cake eaters. Chandeliers dangled from the vaulted ceiling and the amber light of sunset still glowed through stained-glass windows. Aproned waiters bustled back and forth under the hawk-eyed gaze of a maître-d'. And yet, for all this regal charm the old church had an atmosphere of a train station between rush hours.

Suzuki noticed a woman rise from a corner table and advance on her.

'Ms Suzuki?'

Ami Koba was shorter in stature and more compact than she had imagined. She looked like a force to be reckoned with.

'So sorry I'm late,' Suzuki said, mopping her neck and forehead with her handkerchief.

'Don't be silly—it's the heat. It slows us all to a crawl.'

'It certainly does.'

'Will you sit with us?'

Koba led the way, apologizing to the waiting staff as she bulldozed a path across the hall.

On reaching the table, a man placed his napkin down and rose to his feet. Greying, but with a modern hairstyle, he was casually dressed and wore fashionable eyeglasses and a Rolex wristwatch. Suzuki picked him as some kind of self-made businessperson.

'May I introduce Seijiro Hasegawa,' Koba said. 'He's a kannushi, the head priest of Ikuta Shrine.'

Suzuki's eyes betrayed her surprise. The man's clean-shaven face gleamed not from sweat but from good health. His eyebrows, unlike the bristling antenna of most older men, were as neatly clipped as his words. 'A pleasure to meet you, Ms Suzuki.'

'You must be busy. Head priest of the city's most prestigious shrine,' she said.

He smiled modestly. 'As long as there are births and marriages, life will always be so.'

The presence of a Shinto priest in a former Christian church piqued her curiosity. They seated themselves, and after the staff had taken their orders, Koba, lowering her voice, got straight to the point. 'Firstly, thank you for meeting us tonight. My younger sister speaks highly of you.'

Given that she hardly knew Miku Shibata, this remark caused Suzuki to wonder. She smiled politely.

'We have a situation that is both delicate and distressing. It's a very sensitive matter, and we must resolve it in the most discreet way possible. Neither my husband, myself, nor Mr Hasegawa here are sure about how to deal with it and we are wondering if—no, hoping that—you'll help us.'

Suzuki gave a solemn nod. She drew from her handbag her leather-bound notebook and held her pen poised. The staff arrived bearing three iced coffees. They waited until she had left before Koba continued, her voice lowering to a harsh whisper.

'My daughter is twenty-one and a third-year student at Kobe Women's University. She has been working part-time as a *miko*, shrine maiden, at Ikuta Shrine. A few days ago, she told my husband and I that she is pregnant.'

Suzuki's gaze shifted lightly to the priest, who said nothing, and whose face revealed even less.

'On Monday of this week,' Koba continued, 'his *shinshoku*, the novice priest, failed to show. He hasn't been seen since. According to Mr Hasegawa, his mother said he's not been home either. Worse, she's not prepared to discuss the matter.' Her whisper grew harsher. 'My daughter cannot finish her studies. Her career, her marital prospects, family—all ruined.' A tear rolled down her cheek. 'We are worried, confused, devastated....'

Suzuki put down her pen.

'I understand, and I'm sorry you're going through such a difficult time.' Outwardly she maintained her composure, but inside her chest, a sigh the size of a tsunami began to rise. 'I'm afraid I must ask an obvious question. How sure are you that he is the father?'

'My daughter wouldn't lie!' said Koba. A customer seated nearby glanced in their direction. 'The man has fled, for god's sake!' She took a tissue from her pocket and held it to the corners of her eyes. 'I'm sorry. This is just *so* stressful.'

'You would like me to locate him?' It was not a question. Suzuki just wanted to make it easier for her.

But Koba hadn't finished: 'His mother said he has his phone but hasn't made contact. She has no idea where he's gone. I suspect she's lying. We want to find him. We want to talk to him. They will have to marry. My daughter will not be a single mother!'

Suzuki felt a sudden deep, dull pain. It wasn't despair, but it was hurtful. For all the hardship she'd endured as a single mother, no one had ever told her it wasn't possible. Who said that a woman couldn't singlehandedly raise a child—and care for an ageing parent—and still get by, still enjoy life? Single motherhood was rarely a choice, but by the same token, neither was it a curse. The world would not stop turning.

She lifted the glass of iced coffee to her lips, willing the caffeine to revive her, to give her mental strength.

When the priest spoke, his tone was flat and clinical, devoid of emotion. 'Tomoya Nakata is twenty-six-years old. He has apprenticed at Ikuta Shrine for three years. He was hand-selected from the top graduates of Kogakkan University in Mie Prefecture. He is quiet and hard-working, and a very good communicator. He lives with his mother in Rokkomichi. I find his disappearance very troubling and, like Ms Koba, I, too, am in a great state of confusion.'

'Are the police involved?'

Koba shook her head.

'To confirm, he didn't leave a note or a message of any kind?'

'Nothing.'

'May I ask about your daughter?'

'Her name is Sora.'

'Nice name—kanji for sky?'

'Yes.'

'What's she studying at university?'

'She's an English major. She wants to be an airline cabin attendant.'

'Does she still work at the shrine?'

'She will be on duty this Sunday in the shop,' said the priest.

'May I stop by and speak with her?'

The priest glanced at Koba, who nodded and said, 'I'll talk to her tonight.'

'I'll also need to speak with the mother, Ms Nakata?'

'That may not be so easy,' said the priest.

'Oh?'

'She doesn't believe my daughter is telling the truth,' said Koba. 'She thinks her son is being persecuted.'

'But she wants to find her son, doesn't she?'

Ami Koba and the priest exchanged glances. 'I'll call her again tonight,' said the priest.

Memories of the Shimizu case fluttered like a flock of startled crows through Suzuki's mind. Missing-person cases were not only difficult, but they were also unpredictable and exhausting. They took her away from home and family, and there was never any guarantee of a successful outcome. Thus, it all began from zero; the more information she could gather, the easier it would be to decide on whether to accept the case. She gave each of them a detailed list of her services, explaining that any travel beyond Kobe would incur additional costs. It seemed to her, however, that their minds were already made up.

'Mr Hasegawa and my husband and I will share the costs,' Koba said.

'Very well,' Suzuki said, glancing at her watch. 'I have just one more question.' This she directed to the priest. 'Would you say that this young man, Tomoya Nakata, is a trustworthy person?'

A light frown creased his forehead. 'In what sense do you mean?'

'I mean does he take his professional responsibilities seriously?'

'As a novice priest, a *shinshoku* of Ikuta Shrine, he certainly does.'

'Thank you.'

* * *

When Suzuki stepped out into the evening heat, it was as if she were passing between worlds. Her pores gushed. The throbbing in her ankles resumed and she felt suddenly sapped of energy. She shouldered her handbag and rejoined the flow of pedestrians along Flower Road and into Sannomiya.

A pregnant college student and a runaway novice priest. It sounded like a movie. Only, in the film-version the couple usually fled together. Life would always be stranger than fiction. It was why she never took on a missing person's case without conducting her due diligence first.

It wasn't a question of discovering the truth—the missing person *was* the truth—and the reasons why they had disappeared were secondary to knowing where they had disappeared to. Granted, motives sometimes led to surprising discoveries. Such had been the case with Yukihiro Shimizu, whose flight had been guided by nostalgia and a long-lost family connection. However, when it was a case of blind panic caused by the realization that one was about to become a father, impulsive decisions were natural; humans followed their hearts, not their minds. This could make her task as a private investigator a little easier if certain details came to light. Yet, even in possession of these, she had to be wary of making dangerous assumptions. She had to accept that a person might flee with nothing but fear to goad them. In such cases, anything and anywhere was possible. She would have to delve deeper. Right now, her movie had only two characters—and no plot.

* * *

At 7.15 p.m., Sankita Square resembled a circus without a main act. It was a scene one came to expect on any hot summer night, when Kobe's youth rendezvous-ed noisily in the plaza outside Sannomiya train station.

In its midst, Teizo stood reading his pocket paperback. This, she suspected, was just a prop that gave him a respectable right to loiter. It amused her, because anyone reading a book in Sankita Square on a Friday night *was* suspicious!

He wore a short-sleeved shirt with a blue fish pattern, pale jeans, and sand-coloured loafers. A straw hat with a navy-blue band completed his ensemble. His skin was more deeply tanned than she remembered, his silver hair longer and knot-tied behind his hat. He looked like an old rock star, aged gracefully, but far from burnt out.

'Happy birthday, old boy,' she said. 'Nice hat.'

'It was a present to myself.'

'Very sartorial.' She couldn't help but grin as he pocketed his novel. 'No more reading tonight. It's time to party.'

'It happens but once a year.'

Tonight, it was her turn to lead him. They crossed the busy Ikuta-shinmichi Street and entered Kanocho district, where the aromas from steak and seafood restaurants duelled for attention.

Unlike Saturday, with its formalized gatherings and appointed dinner parties, Friday was that one wildcard night of the week when anything could happen. Kokubu, her favourite budget steak restaurant on Kitanozaka Street, would be their starting point, and thereafter, whim would lead the way.

Greeted by staff in kimono and led to the end of a long gleaming grill, they seated themselves at the sunken counter. After the tall-hatted chef had oiled the teppan, presented them with their wagyu fillets and enquired as to how they would like them prepared, Teizo turned to her and said quietly, 'You seem preoccupied.'

She did not want to talk shop, not because her clients' matters were confidential—she trusted him with every detail—but because it would dampen the spirit of their evening. It was his night, and besides, discussing a case before she'd had time to think it through was courting bad luck.

But Teizo could smell a mystery a mile off. He waited patiently until she could do nothing but smile, and say, 'What?'

He was a happy-looking man, and she was happy, too. But he was right, her meeting with Ami Koba and the Shinto priest had ruffled her inner peace. It had been unwise to do business before their long-planned big night out.

Over cold beer, she revealed all. He listened, and when she'd finished his gaze was meditative.

'Long ago,' he said, 'when priests engaged in sex with their shrine maidens, the babies that were born became *mikogami*, children of the gods. Doesn't happen anymore—except by accident. Hence, your runaway novice. What's interesting is that Ikuta Shrine is dedicated to Wakahirume no mikoto, the younger sister of Amaterasu the Sun Goddess. Wakahirume is the deity for creativity and weaving—for matchmaking. She's worshipped for bringing people together.'

'And still doing a great job.'

'You see the paradox, don't you?'

'I do. A perfectly natural act is deemed illicit.'

'What about the girl?'

'We're yet to talk.'

'What did the priest say?'

'Not enough. He seems concerned about the shrine's image. I suspect he fears a scandal.'

'That's ironic.'

'Why?'

'Because Ikuta Shrine has been in the business of getting couples together for eighteen hundred years. Their wedding ceremonies cost a fortune. They're booked solid for a year in advance.'

'How does a retired submariner know all this?'

'Ikuta Shrine houses Daikai Shrine. It's home to Sarutahiko no mikoto, the God of Maritime Safety and Safe Voyages.' He took a sip of beer. 'I also got married there.'

Her gaze returned to the grill. Talk of former marriages, his *or* hers, wasn't a street she felt like ambling down at that moment—not on a night of celebration, not with alcohol in play. The chef returned and the conversation thankfully wheeled back to the heavily marbled steak that he set to grill in front of them. Within moments, it was seared and sliced into bite-sized pieces and placed together with dipping sauces and a side dish of roasted seasonal vegetables.

When their dining was done and the wine bottle emptied, she produced the small ribbon-tied box she had brought with her.

'Happy birthday,' she said, presenting it to him.

Opening it, he exclaimed, 'An earring! But only one?'

She guffawed. 'We'll start you off with one and see how you go.'

He held the Shimano fishing lure to the light, inspecting its rainbow colours and glimmering hook, and said, 'It's perfect. Thank you.'

Later, after departing Kokubu, she led him deeper into Kanocho where the narrow streets of neon-lit bars, clubs, and restaurants turned the night into day. The air grew hotter and louder. She took his arm, and they navigated the crowds of cheerful faces, their own ones coloured by the red lanterns and blue neon sign boards under which they passed.

'Let's sing?' she said.

'Out here?'

'In here.' She tugged him into the garishly lit foyer of Jumbo Karaoke, where knots of office workers and high schoolers came and went from a counter staffed by young men and women in striped waistcoats and straw boater hats.

Riding the lift, Teizo said, 'Did you know that karaoke was invented in Kobe?'

She hiccupped. 'I did not.'

'Back in the seventies there was a bar that wouldn't pay its house musicians on time, so they went on strike. A drummer called Daisuke Inoue felt sorry for his fans so he made a cassette recording of the band's music so customers could sing along to their favourites—without them.'

'Your history lesson is sobering me up,' she croaked. 'Can we just sing?'

The room was small and dark, the air-conditioning icy. They sang songs from their youth, ballads of unrequited love in snowy Hokkaido, anime movie soundtracks, and later, stumbled through half-recalled Simon and Garfunkel and ABBA tunes they had grown up with. They drank more beer and crooned louder, as the city of Kobe made good on its promise in the night beyond.

It was well after midnight when she stepped off the train. Rather than spending money on a taxi home, she mounted her bicycle and wobbled away into the night, sweat-drenched and exhausted beyond belief.

Rounding a corner her eyes widened. She clenched the brakes, setting them screeching. An officer of the Kobe Metropolitan Police stepped into the light.

'Good evening,' he said. He was young with the heavily cauliflowered ears of a judoka or a rugby player. 'Is this your bicycle?'

She nodded.

'Would you please dismount?'

An uptick in theft across the city had prompted her hotel to post memos warning its staff to lock their bicycles securely. Rumour had it that stolen two-wheelers were sold as 'abandoned' to unscrupulous traders who shipped them to Southeast Asia. Teizo's mountain bike had been stolen off the quay a month earlier.

The young officer noted her bicycle's serial number and radioed the details to someone far off. In a few moments, she was free to go. But as she prepared to depart an older officer appeared.

'One moment, please. Have you been drinking?' he asked.

'I attended a birthday party….' Her hiccups were back.

He leant forward. 'Would you breathe on to my face.'

'Pardon me?'

'Breathe, please.'

It was city policing the old school way. Nevertheless, she did as she was told, knowing it better to comply than to lock horns with the Kobe Metropolitan Police. She blew and he sniffed. He nodded, turned around and said something to his subordinate.

'Would you please blow in this?' the young officer said, producing a small device.

She blew until dizzy, until Old School said, 'that'll do' and took the breathalyser from her. He shook his head, clicking his tongue. 'Article 2, Item 11 of the Road Traffic Law states that riding a bicycle while intoxicated is against the law.' He showed her the reading. 'But you knew that didn't you?'

She could only bow her head and hiccupped, 'I'm sor-ry.'

Her driver's licence was requested, notes were taken.

'The maximum penalty for *in-shu-unten* is one-million yen and up to five years' imprisonment.'

'I'm….' She repressed a hiccup. 'I'm very sorry.'

Had it been Old School by himself, she might have wiggled her way out of it. But with a junior officer present, an example had to be set. She watched grimly as he scribbled into his pad, tore off a docket, and handed it to her with her licence.

'A warning. Please pay at City Hall.'

Beneath the dull glow of the streetlight, she stared at the number on the paper. She wanted to burst into tears. No amount of sobbing and pleading would change the situation, and in a few moments another cyclist rounded the corner, his brakes also squealing. The officers moved on, leaving her to wheel her bicycle off into the darkness.

* * *

Saturday morning was a write off.

To salvage something of the afternoon, she took her daughter to the cinema and in its cool depths, with Doraemon the earless cat flickering across the screen, she fell asleep. She was woken by the theatre staff sweeping the aisle, her daughter dozing in the chair beside her, covered in caramel popcorn.

Back at the apartment she drank a long glass of chilled barley tea. Then, she took out the four cans of beer from the refrigerator, and together with the half-bottle of whisky and a box of convenience store Chardonnay, she carried them into the laundry and placed them in the high cupboard reserved for cleaning liquids and other dangerous solvents. For good measure, she firmly affixed the childproof lock; all this while her mother watched on silently.

The drink-riding penalty would cost dearly. More worrying, it now left her no choice; she'd have to take the case of the runaway novice priest on its flimsy merits. Fate had decided for her.

She entered her room and shut the door. There she buried her head in her futon pillow and cried.

* * *

Although she couldn't yet see it for the office towers and department stores lining Ikuta Street, she could hear its deep, bellowing drum. Then came the wailing skirl of a *kami-oroshi no fue*, the 'flute that calls gods', and she wondered how it had come to be that an 1,800-year-old Shinto shrine should still be standing in the heart of one of Japan's most vibrant and modern port cities.

It had been years since she'd paid a visit to Ikuta Shrine. The early days of the New Year were out of the question—the crowds stretched around an entire city block.

It was now almost 5 p.m., and a steady flow of Sunday worshippers and tourists drifted along the smooth stone pathway to the shrine's main entrance.

The previous day, a text message from the priest, Hasegawa, had arrived informing her that Sora Koba, with the consent of her parents, would meet with her after her shift had ended.

Suzuki paused to mop her face and neck. Dressed not so much for an austere meeting with a shrine maiden as for surviving a steamy July afternoon, she wore a white cotton shirt, loose linen pants in indigo, and her black A.Emery sandals.

Beyond the gate, two figures crossed the pebbled forecourt and climbed the steps of the haiden, the worshipping hall of Ikuta Shrine. Their long dark hair fastened at the back, red *hakama* skirts, and white cloaks marked them as *miko*—maidens of the shrine.

It was common knowledge that during the busy periods of New Year and Children's Day, these jobs were filled by part-timers, usually university students, and involved basic administrative tasks such as staffing the amulet shop counter and assisting the priest. As a student, Suzuki herself had been offered one, but had turned it down for the better pay of a yaki-tori restaurant.

She glanced at her watch.

'Ms Suzuki?'

The voice startled her. She turned around to find a young woman of medium height, average build and normal appearance watching her. She wore jeans, sneakers, and an orange T-shirt with a Bathing Ape insignia across the chest.

'Sora?'

The young woman managed a smile.

Sensing her awkwardness, Suzuki said quickly, 'Shall we walk? The forest looks peaceful today.'

Ikuta Shrine was famous for its garden—an expansive grove of ancient yew, oak, and camphor trees through which a small stream sidled. Here, worshippers and city workers sought solace and refuge during the week. Together the two women climbed the path, passed by its pond filled with yellow lotus flowers and entered its sacred glade.

The hubbub of the shrinegoers faded into bird calls and the soughing of a light breeze in the canopy overhead. Here and there, pathways branched off to smaller shrines dedicated to various other deities. She wondered which one led to Teizo's God of Maritime Safety and Safe Voyages.

When they reached a small gazebo, they sat.

'Firstly, congratulations,' Suzuki said. 'It *is* customary to congratulate a woman on her pregnancy.'

Sora Koba smiled weakly. 'It's funny, isn't it.'

'What is?'

'Miko are supposed to be virgins.'

'Well, that's the official line … I doubt anyone cares.'

'What's it like to be a detective?'

Suzuki laughed. 'Well, I'm more of a researcher. I gather information to help people…. In this case, information about Tomoya Nakata. There are people who want to find him— yourself included, am I right?'

Koba's face was as featureless as a desert.

'You *do* want to find him, don't you?' Suzuki repeated.

'Yes.'

It was the least convincing 'affirmative' Suzuki had ever heard. 'Can I start with the big one? Has Tomoya contacted you at all since he disappeared? And just to be clear, anything you say remains between just the two of us.'

'No.'

'Have you tried to contact him?'

'I've sent him messages. I know he reads them, but he never replies.'

'Any idea where he might have gone?'

'He loves cats.'

'Sorry?'

'Cats. He's always wanted a cat, but his mother is allergic to them.'

Suzuki took a mental step back. 'How might that help me to find him?'

'I don't know. It's the only thing that came to mind.'

Suzuki penned 'cats' in her notebook. She'd run with that. 'If he wants a cat, why doesn't he move out of home?'

'Because he doesn't want to leave her alone. His father died when he was young. He's an only child—like me.'

'But he *has* left her alone. He's disappeared.'

'He'll be back.'

'When?'

'I don't know.' The words tumbled out, dazed and hopeless sounding, as if their speaker had been the sole survivor of a plane crash and was being asked by rescuers what had happened?

Suzuki sucked in the warm moist air, thick with pungent odours of rotting leaves, and breathed out.

'May I ask—what kind of person is Tomoya?'

'What do you mean?'

'Is he confident? Shy? Impulsive? Happy-go-lucky? Serious…? '

'Serious.'

Suzuki added the word; that made two. 'What about travel? Adventurous—an outdoorsy type? Does he drive, ride a motorbike….'

She shook her head. 'He likes trains. Driving stresses him.'

Suzuki looked at the three words in her notebook. 'Do you have any reason to believe he might still be in the Kobe area?'

'I don't know.'

'Did he ever talk about the future? About places he'd like to visit?'

The young woman's gaze fell to her sneakers and lingered there. 'He asked me if I'd like to visit a cat island,' she said after a while.

'What's a cat island?'

'An island where the cats run free, where you can pet them, photograph them, cuddle them....'

Suzuki's pen picked up the pace. 'Where is this cat island?'

'It's not one. There are several. In the Seto Inland Sea, I think. He didn't tell me their names; I don't even think he knew himself. He just wanted to visit one of them with me.'

'Sounds like an interesting guy.'

Koba turned and faced her. There was a strange desperation in her eyes. Suzuki could not know its source, but she'd seen it before. It was the look of a fallen angel, a shrine maiden whom the Shinto gods had abandoned, and it unsettled her.

'There's one final question I'd like to ask,' Suzuki said. 'It's about the nature of your....' She caught herself. Tears had welled in Koba's eyes. 'I'm sorry. Another time.'

'What is it?'

'I just want to ask how long you've been seeing each other—I mean, as boyfriend and girlfriend?'

'He's not my boyfriend.' She sniffed and wiped her eyes.

'Okay, then how would you describe your relationship?'

'He's my *senpai*—my senior.'

'Do you love each other?' It was a risky question, but she had to chance it. The answer might determine the range Nakata was prepared, or not prepared, to travel.

'I do.'

'And him?'

'I don't know.'

Suzuki sensed the young woman's exhaustion. She'd have to settle for what she'd gleaned so far. 'Thank you for sharing with me. I'm sorry if I've upset you in any way.'

'Let me show you something,' Koba said, rising from her seat. She led Suzuki down the path, across the meandering stream and between a stand of giant yews, before arriving at a small pond. A sign beside it read: *En-musubi no mizu-uranai*, 'water fortune-telling for matchmaking'.

The young woman took from her pocket two pink-coloured sheaves of paper. 'Are you married, Ms Suzuki?'

'I was once.'

'Would you like to join me then?' She handed one of the papers to her. 'Lay it in the water and your horoscope will appear.'

Suzuki hesitated. Not out of fear, but out of her intense dislike of fortune-telling. 'Here goes nothing,' she muttered, and followed Koba's lead, placing the paper on to the pond's surface. A moment passed. Slowly, like an old-fashioned photo developer, a message materialized. She lifted it out and let the water drain away.

'*You are loved more than you know*'.

True—for almost every human on Earth. What had she expected? 'Error 404: Fortune Not Found'?

'Any luck?' she asked. Koba shook her head and folded the damp paper into a taper, stepped to a small pine tree which stood beside the pool and tied it to a branch. 'It's best to leave your bad fortune here, so it won't follow you home.'

'Who writes these things?' asked Suzuki, following her lead.

'I don't know.'

* * *

That evening, Suzuki sat at her kitchen table thinking about how much she would love a cold beer.

But there was none—and there would be none. Not until her situation improved. She got up, walked to the refrigerator, and peered inside. She took out a bottle of soda water, filled a glass with ice, and squeezed in a jet of yuzu syrup. Stirring it with a fork, she resumed her seat in front of the glowing screen of her ageing laptop.

The apartment was quiet.

Her mother and daughter were sound asleep next-door, and only the lingering smell of steamed gyoza remained of the family dinner. On the table, her notebook page, a collection of keywords and Sora Koba's quote that she'd penned in afterward: 'I don't know.' It was the one thing they had in common. It was how all investigations began. The leads, though seemingly random, were strengthening. A picture was forming of a young man in a temporary state of anxiety, fleeing his responsibility as a father-to-be, and his spiritual duties as a novice priest at Kobe's oldest and most prestigious Shinto shrine. A young man who needed time to think—on an island of cats?

Her fingers danced over the worn keys and in a few moments, she was staring at three candidates:

Tashirojima, Miyagi Prefecture, north-eastern Honshu

Aoshima, Ehime Prefecture, Shikoku Island

Manabeshima, Okayama Prefecture, western Honshu

At first glance, Aoshima seemed to be the favourite; a tiny island with a population of six people, all over the age of seventy-five and living among more than two hundred cats, thirty minutes by ferry from Shikoku Island. She viewed the photos of tourists besieged by hungry felines, scattering pet biscuits, patting, petting, smiling—happy. From Kobe, one could cross the Akashi Bridge and enter Shikoku by way of Awaji Island, then follow the highway through Tokushima Prefecture to the eastern end of Ehime Prefecture, a driving distance of approximately 320 kilometres. There was only one problem: no accommodation was available for visitors to the island.

Tashirojima, on the other hand, offered lodgings. It had a curious history; the island was once home to a thriving silk farming industry. To keep its worm-eating mice population in check, cats had been introduced. End of story. Located almost one thousand kilometres from Kobe, however, it would be a determined cat lover who would travel that kind of distance to pet a cat.

Manabeshima, like Aoshima, lay in the Seto Inland Sea. At 220 kilometres from Kobe, it was the closest. The Shimizu case had taken her as far as Kurashiki; Kasaoka lay only a short distance beyond.

Tomoya Nakata was not a fan of driving, according to Koba. Suzuki pulled up the ferry timetable, which showed eight crossings daily from Kasaoka to Manabeshima that lay thirty kilometres away. Its population of eighty-three people was outnumbered two-to-one by cats.

Manabeshima or Aoshima?

She had two contenders, two islands overrun by cats that were both within easy reach by rail and ferry lines from Kobe. Only one of them—Manabeshima—offered accommodation.

She glanced at the wall clock. Almost 10 p.m.

How she craved a can of beer. There was a 7-Eleven just down the street. She forced the convenience store demon from her mind and reached for Hasegawa's business card. She wondered if Shinto priests were night owls. She needed an audience with Nakata's mother, and he was yet to get back to her.

All at once her phone vibrated, the caller's number identical to the one on the card in her hand.

'Hello?'

'Ms Suzuki?'

'Mr Hasegawa?'

'Sorry to call you at this hour.'

'How bizarre—I was about to call you.'

'Ami Koba mentioned you work at the Orient Hotel? Can I meet you in the cafe there after work tomorrow?'

'Do you know Port Tower Cafe?'

'Yes.'

'I'll meet you there at 6 p.m.' She paused. 'May I ask what the matter is?'

'Nakata has contacted me.'

* * *

She awoke feeling refreshed. Was her teetotalling paying dividends already?

The day passed quickly; a Chinese cruise ship party kept the hotel front desk busy with requests for room changes, lost keys, and Mandarin-speaking staff to deal with more challenging issues. On top of this, she had to contend with Goto buzzing about like an annoying fruit fly, making suggestions, interrupting conservations, and worst of all, admonishing her in front of guests.

With great relief she pushed on the staff entrance door and stepped out into the fug of the early evening. She made her way along the esplanade to the Port Tower, entered the lobby and took the lift to the top floor.

Funny, she thought—she passed Port Tower five days a week, yet could count the times on one hand that she'd actually stepped inside its revolving skyline cafe. Tonight, the window-side counter rotated soundlessly, taking a handful of customers on a 360-degree bird's eye tour of Kobe, from the Rokko mountains to the Inland Sea.

Hasegawa was seated with his back to her; his sweat-darkened pink polo shirt said he'd just arrived, and it pleased her to know that she wasn't alone in suffering the heat.

At her approach, he rose to greet her. He seemed more anxious than at their first meeting at the church cafe. They seated themselves, and after ordering iced coffees, he got straight to the point.

'Nakata telephoned me yesterday afternoon. He said he wants to quit his apprenticeship.'

'Did he say where he is?'

'No.'

'What else?'

'He's sorry for the trouble he has caused.'

'That's all?'

'That's all.'

The iced coffee arrived and the furrows on Hasegawa's brow deepened. Stirring in cream and syrup, he said, 'He is a hard-working, talented novice. Immensely talented! I can't afford to lose him.' He drank without pleasure. He turned to her. 'May I ask—do you have any leads?'

'Only possibilities.'

'Then I'd like to make a special request.'

Her eyebrows arched. 'Yes?'

'When you find him, persuade him to return to the shrine. There are people who need him.'

'Sora Koba comes to mind.'

'Yes, yes, of course, but I mean the community, too. The City of Kobe!'

'I appreciate that our most venerated shrine is eager to have their *shinshoku* return, but as I've said, a concrete lead is yet to materialize. Furthermore, psycho-persuasion isn't part of my skill set....'

'Oh, but I think it is, Ms Suzuki.' He leant towards her, his eyes widening. 'I think you have a way with people that makes them receptive to change.'

She wondered what he meant by the remark. It smelt of desperation.

'Thank you for the kind words but making contact with the subject of a missing person's case is never in my terms.'

'Why not?'

'There are legal issues—and it's also dangerous.'

She tried to sound resolute, but her words felt hollow. How often did cases conclude *because* of a face-to-face encounter? A pearl thief saved from herself, a missing sushi chef reconnected with his family, a dead man's sister appeased.... She might go as far as to venture that it even determined a case's success. Of course, she had never to remind herself of the dangers inherent in confronting a desperate individual.

But this time, the desperation was in the priest's eyes.

'What you're asking me to do will change my fee structure,' she said.

'Understood.'

'Fifty per cent—plus expenses. I can adjust the contract.'

'A separate one, if you don't mind. And may we keep this between us?'

'You mean...?'

'I'd rather the Koba family didn't know.'

That humans moved in mysterious ways would always keep her in business. That the sun would always rise in the east would keep her sane. The cafe had completed one revolution. She had watched the world pass her by: first the Orient Hotel, then the Mosaic Shopping Mall with its Ferris wheel, the Kawasaki shipyards and submarine docks, next the featureless urban sprawl which stretched all the way to the hills of Suma, and beyond this, the green and blue strobing lights of the Akashi Bridge. Now, as they embarked on a second orbit, she glimpsed something she'd hadn't really taken the time to appreciate. It was the illuminated anchor that stood high on the Rokko mountainside, the symbol of the City of Kobe, the one true constant which never stopped shining.

'I'll still need to talk with his mother,' she said.

'That was the other reason I wanted to meet. She won't meet you.'

'Did she give a reason?'

'Same as before—she believes Sora Koba is lying.'

'What do you think?'

'I don't know what to think.' His gaze swung back to the harbour. 'It's really none of my business.'

It was the kind of remark a doctor would make and it irritated her. Medicines, not opinions, were easier to dole out. Treat the symptom and not the cause. She highly doubted the extra fee he was offering for a 'good dose of persuasiveness' would return his novice priest, even if she was able to determine his whereabouts.

She felt the muscles in her neck tightening, a headache building. Nearby, an elderly customer had taken a seat and now a frosted tumbler of beer sat before him. She watched as he lifted it to his lips, and like a parched desert reptile, swallowed the cold beer in big, noisy gulps.

She looked away.

A week without alcohol was her personal record, and she was breaking it daily. Abstaining had done wonders for her hip pocket, even her productivity, but at that very moment, with the heat of the night pressing against the windowpane, she craved a chilled glass of beer more than anything else on earth. Her gaze roamed the cafe for a waiter.

'I'm afraid I must leave,' Hasegawa said, suddenly. He collected the bill and rose from his seat. 'Without Nakata, I'm barely managing at the shrine.'

'Yes, of course. Thank you,' she said, collecting her bag. 'I just have one final last question.'

'Yes?'

'Did anything strike you as strange during your call with him?'

'You mean his manner?'

'I mean background noise—did you hear anything unusual?'

He regarded her oddly for a moment. 'Nothing. Why?'

'Just a line of inquiry I'm working on.'

They took the lift, but she waited for him to depart before making her way back to the train station. Just before the ticket gate, her phone vibrated. She stepped quickly into an alcove. 'Mr Hasegawa?'

'I've been thinking,' he said.

'Yes?'

'There *was* something strange about the call.'

She waited.

'Nakata usually speaks quietly…. There was a sound like crying in the background.'

'Human?'

'Not human.'

'Animal? Like a cat meowing?'

A pause. 'Yes, come to think of it. Like many cats meowing.'

* * *

A strong onshore breeze blew as she stepped off the train in Kasaoka. Gripping her hat, she rolled her suitcase through the pedestrian underpass and emerged onto a shopping street that time had forgotten. Stores on each side stood forlorn and shuttered, their rusted signs advertising brands that no longer existed. Loose iron sheeting clanged in the wind and an empty beer car leapt and tumbled ahead of her.

Kasaoka was a small inland sea town famous for chicken ramen and horseshoe crabs—if the train station tourism brochure was to be believed. She saw evidence of neither as she pressed on for the port.

Teizo could have told her more if she'd asked. But she hadn't because she didn't want him involved in the case. It was a weak argument, of course. He was her most trusted source of information, reasoning, and logical thought. Deep down, she knew it was the embarrassment of being caught drink-cycling on the night of his birthday that she couldn't face. Besides, every time they met it was always over a bottle, and she had made a promise to herself to quit drinking—until a good reason to celebrate showed itself.

Like Kasaoka itself, the ferry terminal was a salt-stained concrete relic from a previous Emperor's reign. After purchasing a ticket, she waited in the bare departure hall, reviewing her notes and half-watching the passengers who came and went through the pier gates.

They were shorter, stockier than Kobe city folk; their calloused hands, muscled forearms, and weathered faces spoke of a different lifestyle. Some of the men wore old-fashioned trilby hats, the women bonnets; their unpretentious sun-faded

clothes lending them a timeless look, like extras in a period
TV drama.

Travellers ebbed and flowed, and through the window
Suzuki watched their piles of boxes and cartons rise and fall
with every boat departure from the pier.

When her call to board came, she joined the solemn
procession down the gangway to the waiting ferry, but rather
than take a seat inside the cabin, she joined a young couple and
their son on the deck at the rear.

In a few moments, the floor gave a horrible shudder as
diesel fumes belched and billowed and the propeller tore
at the green harbour water. They motored out through a
channel, following its muddy banks past ramshackle fisher
huts and flocks of cormorants whose drying wings reminded
Suzuki of fake watch salesmen, until Kasaoka was nothing
more than a grey smudge against the lumpy green hills of the
Okayama hinterland.

Entering the Seto Inland Sea proper, the captain opened the
throttle and a fine spray swept over her, cool and tangy to taste.
She gripped her hat, squinting into the distance. On a map, the
Kasaoka Island group resembled a handful of shrapnel—the
result of an epic volcanic explosion millennia ago that had sent
magna hurtling across western Japan. And yet, passing their tiny
golden beaches rimmed by smooth boulders and lush native
forest, they seemed almost paradisiacal.

A short while later, the cabin door swung open and a squat
man in blue work wear stepped out to collect their tickets.

'Shark!' cried the boy, pointing out to sea.

The ticket man chuckled. 'That's a harbour porpoise, kid.
You're lucky to see one.'

Shielding her eyes against the glare, Suzuki caught sight of
a pale grey form sliding smoothly away from the bow. Though

she wasn't superstitious, she'd happily take any good omen in the offing right now.

Was she confident of finding Tomoya Nakata?

No—

But like a water diviner, she would feel her way forwards, intuition guiding her, not knowing exactly what would transpire or what awaited around the next corner but resolute in her belief that if you fell down seven times, you got up eight. There was never any certainty with cases like these, only hunches based on loose facts which, when arranged, pointed in a general direction.

That direction was now Manabeshima—the last in Kasaoka's group of seven islands.

Presently, the captain announced their approach to Konoshima. On to the island's wooden pier, the young boy and his parents disembarked, juggling suitcases and fishing rods, until they were lost to the sea spray as the ferry powered onwards.

The islands of Takashima, Shiraishijima, Kitagi, Kitaura, and Mushima came and went. The swell grew higher and the shipping lanes busier. Container vessels and bulk carriers slid silently across the horizon, fishing boats bucked and bobbed across their bow, and now and then, a yacht with its main sail straining eased between the islands. Though the sun shone, the high clouds streaked the sky like strips of torn cloth. The wind was strengthening.

Gazing back at Honshu, she wondered why anyone would travel thirty kilometres from the safety of the mainland just to pet cats. Was it because city people lived in apartments too small, or too unfriendly, to keep pets? Or was it simply the novelty and adventure of travelling by boat to a 'cat island' that wooed them?

That was another question for Tomoya Nakata.

She had spent the morning train ride from Kobe delving deeper into the cat connection, scrolling breeds, trends, myths and legends, even allergy remedies. Cats were mysterious creatures, revered, and even feared in the olden times. Not that she was a fan. They were selfish beasts, with shifty eyes, sharp teeth, and claws good only for shredding wallpaper and laddering upholstery. In winter they hogged the heater, in summer they were nowhere to be seen. Their hair got in everything.

Suzuki had also taken the opportunity to refresh her knowledge of *bake-neko*, the spirit cat, whose tales all children grew up hearing and fearing. With imagination applied, a storyteller could turn the common feline into a malevolent member of the *yokai* world of ghosts, ghouls, and goblins, which stalked the night, brutally killing and eating humans. She had to admit, it was otherwise useless information, but should she meet Nakata it might prove useful currency.

Across the racing whitecaps, Suzuki now discerned an island. The captain throttled down and soon the ferry nosed gently towards Honmura, the largest of Manabeshima's two villages. It might have been a movie set for a samurai flick, like the one in Kyoto, with its tiled roofed houses and white-washed earthen walls, all clustered together like a colony of beetles on the leeward side of the island. Above the village ran a low ridgeline patch-worked with kitchen gardens and fruit trees that the wind wrestled back and forth.

As the ferry entered between the breakwater, Suzuki strained her eyes, searching the foreshore for signs of life.

For a while nothing moved.

Then a curious thing happened.

A flotilla of fishing boats overtook them, and as it motored into port, the shorefront suddenly came to life. What might have been bollards, octopus pots, or piles of old rope, were all at once animated. Coloured ginger, white, black, piebald, with long tails and tails missing, old and young, sickly and strong, creatures leapt and bounded towards the dock where the fishing boats now prepared to throw out their mooring lines.

The harbour master appeared at the end of the ferry pier, and together with his two assistants, secured the boat and drew up the gangway for the disembarking passengers.

Suzuki stepped on to the creaking dock, and with suitcase in tow, made for a row of ancient shops behind the seawall. Phone reception was weak, but she had come prepared. Pausing to consult her print-out of Honmura, she realized she was standing outside its only restaurant. It was almost noon. If Tomoya Nakata *was* on Manabeshima, it was unlikely he'd be going anywhere soon.

Suddenly, she felt hungry.

* * *

The restaurant was called Umi-no-resutoran, Sea Restaurant, and she hoped its offerings might be more imaginative than its name. Inside, the place was a jumble of homely chaos. A raised floor with worn tatami mats offered space for a small party of diners. It was as if she'd entered someone's kitchen as the sole diner.

'Gomen-kudasai! Hello?' she called.

No reply came.

A large ginger cat slinked through the doorway, giving her no more than a cursory glance as it sniffed the air. It padded across the room to the raised floor where the remains of a light lunch still sat on the low table, leapt on to the tatami and stood on its hind legs, nostrils flaring over the oily dishes. It began lapping at one of them.

'Gomen-kudasai! Hello?' Suzuki called louder. The cat looked up sharply.

Soon an elderly woman appeared through the curtained rear door. With a vile hiss, she shooed the cat away, and said, 'Hello, dear. I didn't expect many more customers today.'

'Oh? Why's that?

She gave Suzuki a curious look. 'Typhoon number seven is on its way.'

'I thought that was heading for Korea.'

'You didn't hear? It changed course. Weather report says it's going to hit western Honshu tomorrow morning.'

Suzuki's eyebrows rose. 'Tomorrow?'

She hadn't bothered to check the news since the previous night, so engrossed in her research had she been until now.

'You'll be spending the weekend on the island then?'

'No, I was hoping to be away sooner.'

The woman frowned. 'I'm sorry, dear, but the last ferry for Kasaoka is leaving now.'

'What?'

'They're suspending the service until Monday morning.'

Cold panic swept through her. Without a word, she leapt through the doorway tugging her suitcase and ran as fast as she could along the foreshore. The ferry was still there, its exhaust bubbling and a handful of passengers sitting inside the cabin.

A wheel fell off her suitcase. She cursed. Tomoya Nakata or no—she wasn't going to weather a typhoon on a far-flung island in the Seto Inland Sea. She hurried on, dragging the bouncing valise behind her.

'Wait!' she cried, but a gust of wind stole her words. When she reached the dock, the harbour master had just cast the last mooring rope into the hands of a crew member.

'Wait! Wait!'

The harbour master turned, his eyes wide at the sight of the panicked woman dragging her broken suitcase.

'Is that the last boat?' she gasped.

'To Kasaoka? Yes, it is….'

She abandoned the suitcase and ran to the end of the pier, in time to glimpse the ferry's cabin door open and a man step on to the rear deck. He stood at the rails gazing back at the village. He was youthful looking with dark hair and sunlight glinting off his glasses.

'Tomoya Nakata! Tomoya Nakata!' She waved vigorously.

But the man seemed not to hear—or comprehend.

She could only stand at the tip of the pier and watch as the pilot guided the boat out through the breakwater and launched it into the pale green maelstrom. The young man turned and went inside.

'Shit!'

She had broken the private investigator's golden rule: always follow the changing dynamic. Any public address announcement, overheard conversation, or chalkboard notice pertaining to weather or ferry schedules, had been missed. She'd even forgotten to pack an umbrella! Not that it would be of any use in a typhoon, but that was beside the point now.

If it had been Tomoya Nakata staring back at her from the ferry's deck then he was a lot smarter than her.

She took out her phone. There were calls to be made.

* * *

'Look at it this way, you've got the run of the island,' smiled the old matron back at the Sea Restaurant.

Suzuki glanced at the saucer the cat had licked clean, still lying on the table.

'Does that cat usually do that?' she asked.

'Do what, dear?'

'Help himself to your food. That one who was licking fish oil off the plate ...'

'He's a serial offender. There'll be hell to pay if I catch him doing it again.' She scooped up the dirty dishes and deposited them with a clatter into the kitchen basin.

'Do you believe in bake-neko?'

The woman chuckled. 'No. Do you?'

'No. It's just that in Edo times, a bake-neko licking lamp oil while standing on its hind legs was an omen said to forewarn of a catastrophic event.'

The old woman looked thoughtful. 'Yes, I seem to recall hearing that too....' She shrugged and looked at Suzuki as if to ask her point. But there was none. To say that typhoon number seven was going to pummel Manabeshima just because a greedy cat had hoovered up a saucer of sardine oil would be a longshot even by any fortune teller's measure!

She ordered yaki-soba, and after eating it quickly, paid her bill and left the Sea Restaurant feeling utterly despondent.

* * *

The guesthouse owner was consoling. But not for reasons Suzuki would have thought.

'It's such a shame about the weather,' the kindly middle-aged woman said. 'You won't be able to pet the cats.' She guided her to a large room beside a small garden at the back of the traditional wood and tile-roofed homestead.

'Were you busy last night?' asked Suzuki.

'I had three guests.'

'From Kobe?'

'Two were university students from Nagoya—and one *very* nice young man from somewhere near Kobe....'

'Rokkomichi?'

'Yes, yes, that's right!' The woman looked at her curiously. 'Is he a friend of yours?'

'If it's the person I'm thinking of, then we are mutually acquainted. He's a cat lover, I believe?'

'He certainly is—and a *real* gentleman, too.' She clapped her hands gleefully. 'Such a small world, isn't it?'

'It certainly is.' Suzuki forced a smile, but the irony made her want to cry.

She felt her phone vibrate.

Apologizing, she stepped through the veranda doors and into the small garden. Low clouds scudded by overhead; the sun shone brightly between them, and the breeze was warm and briny in her face.

'Mr Goto? You received my message?' She cringed. 'Yes. Yes. Thank you so much. My family deeply appreciates your condolences at this time. Yes. The funeral is on Monday, and I will be back at work on Tuesday morning. Once again, sorry for your inconvenience.'

She waited until he'd hung up, before exhaling. Sometimes the death of an imaginary uncle came in handy. Only, one had to be careful not to kill them off too frequently.

Her mother had been less accommodating. Their conversation had started with the usual, 'I can't find my glasses' and ended with 'So, you'll be home for dinner tomorrow?'

Patience was a virtue in short supply during such long-distance conversations, but Suzuki managed to make it clear that she would now be spending two nights on Manabeshima and that the imminent typhoon would be no more than—to use the Sea Restaurant matron's words—'a patch of bad weather'. She would see her and Aya on Monday evening. As for her reading glasses, they were right where they always were—on top of her mother's head!

No sooner had she hung up than her phone vibrated again. 'Yes?'

Hasegawa greeted her. His tone was cautious. 'Has Ami Koba contacted you yet?'

'I tried her earlier. The line was busy.'

'Then you don't know?'

'Know what?'

'Nakata's not the father.'

'What?'

'Sora Koba admitted everything to her parents this morning. She says she's sorry for the trouble she's caused.'

'I'm sorry—could you say that again?'

'Sora Koba and Tomoya Nakata never had sex. The girl was lying.'

For a moment the world inside her head sounded very loud. *Sorry for the trouble she's caused* clanged like a temple bell, but with far less cheer.

Hasegawa explained: Ami Koba had called him two hours earlier, but he only found out a few minutes ago that Nakata had left Manabeshima—his novice had called to tell him so. Hasegawa was sorry.

Suzuki remained silent.

What did it matter if Nakata was now disembarking on the mainland, about to board an air-conditioned train bound for Kobe, to see his mother and eat her dinner in the safe comfort of his own home in Rokkomichi? What did it matter that Hasegawa would stand by his offer to pay in full the agreed-on extra fee? What did it matter that she had done all the hard work—only to be the last person to learn the truth?

She wanted to shake her fist at the sky. She wanted to scream at the gods like a crazed woman. Instead, she said, 'Thank you,' and hung up.

She was still angry when she punched Ami Koba's number a moment later. She was angrier when the woman's messaging machine activated; and angry beyond belief when her phone battery died halfway through her message.

The wind blew with greater ferocity. It forced her from the garden and back inside her room where it wailed and whinnied, seeking out cracks and crevices in the homestead's earthen walls. Despite the humidity, Suzuki shivered.

A flask of barley tea, a cup, and a small cake had been placed on the low table. She tugged on the ceiling light cord, but nothing happened. She inserted her phone charging cord into the wall socket, but nothing happened. She sat down and quietly drank her tea and ate her sweet in the darkened room. Nothing happened.

'Don't worry,' said the guesthouse owner later. 'It's just a temporary outage. The transformer on Takashima sometimes shuts down in bad weather. Besides, we have a diesel generator. You can power your phone off it tonight if you like?'

'Any sooner?'

'Is it an emergency?'

'No…,' she said wearily.

'Well then, make yourself at home. Relax.' As she turned to leave, Suzuki stopped her.

'Can you tell me—where do all the cats go in a typhoon?'

'You know,' she said, 'I've often wondered that myself.'

* * *

The typhoon arrived that evening.

Not as a careening freight train might, but as a tussle of air currents that grew ever more violent as the night wore on.

She lay on her sweat-dampened futon, hardly hearing the putter of the diesel generator beneath the roar of the gale, hoping that the roof tiles wouldn't flutter away and leave her at the mercy of the Wind God, *Fujin*. The paper doors rattled like old bones in their grooves. The storm shutters puffed in and out like a concertina. A fine, almost invisible dust filled the air each time the ceiling timbers shook and flexed.

She was completely alone.

The guesthouse owner, residing in the building adjacent, had ageing parents to care for. There was no mention, or sign, of any husband. Suzuki hadn't bothered to ask.

She rolled from her futon, poured some tea from the flask, and wondered about the other denizens of Manabeshima. The harbour master, the Sea Restaurant matron, the fishers ... what were they all doing at that very moment?

And where were the cats?

The rain hammered against the outside walls. Sometimes, it felt as if a giant were lifting the house off its foundations and shaking it like a pod containing a single pea. The ceiling light dimmed and wavered with the pulsing of the generator current, but soon her phone was charged.

To her disbelief, there was no signal.

She lay on her futon, passing the night fitfully, tossing and turning, unable to sleep, unable to think, unable to contact the outside world. Other times she thought she heard an animal cry, a thin piercing wail which reached into her half-dreams. Wind, woman, or cat? She couldn't be sure about anything anymore.

Hunkered in the lee, Honmura weathered the gale; its tiled roof armour fending off the thrashing wind and rain, its denizens stoic and stubborn, unflinching in the face of *Fūjin* as they had been for centuries.

Dawn brought with it a strange calm. The roar of the wind had gone but through the walls came other sounds: a hammer striking iron, the whine of an electric drill, and the hum of a small truck navigating the narrow alley in front of the guest house.

'You survived!' The owner greeted her with a smile at the breakfast table. 'Good news. There'll be a ferry arriving this afternoon. The sea isn't as rough as expected. That is, unless you'd like to stay until Monday?' Her smile faded. 'Is something the matter?'

Suzuki's face was pale and sleepless. In her hand, she held her phone. Reception had been restored and with it had come a deluge of messages. Four from Ami Koba, two from her mother, two from Hasegawa, one from Teizo—and one from Goto.

It was the last one she now read:

It has come to my attention that you are currently not experiencing a death in the family, but are, for all intents and purposes, engaged in a second job. As you are aware, the Kobe Orient Hotel prides itself on the honesty and loyalty of its staff, and while your service years total longer than my own, you have left me no choice but to inform the directors of your misdeed.

Suzuki looked up. 'I'm sorry, what did you say?'

'I said, the ferry will be arriving this afternoon … are you alright?'

She nodded vacantly. Her gaze fell to the final word in Goto's missive.

Misdeed.

It had a dullness to it, like a blunt instrument used for bludgeoning fish, only this one cut deep.

'I'm quite alright, thank you.'

She placed her phone down, picked up her chopsticks and began eating. Only after the woman had left the room did she allow the tears to flow.

* * *

The ferry arrived a little after 3 p.m.

It crept in through the debris-filled harbour like a wary workhorse, its deckhands busy with pushing away anything that might snare the propeller, while the harbour master communicated to the pilot using hand signals.

The ferry dock had been spared. The fishing fleet had suffered only superficial damage; miraculously, not one of its vessels had been lost.

Aboard the ferry, Suzuki deposited her suitcase inside the cabin and stepped on to the stern deck. She gazed back at Honmura's shorefront, at its timbered and tiled shophouses, darkened and wet, but otherwise standing firm. Along the sea wall and the piers, she saw no sign of any cats.

Except for one—its ginger body bobbed among the detritus of the harbour—drifting gently away in the bow wash of the ferry as it passed.

Once beyond the breakwater, the warm sea breeze pressed against her skin, not foetid and suffocating as before, but clear and sweet, as if purged of all impurities. Beneath the harsh glare of the sun, she watched Manabeshima grow smaller, until the ridgeline melded with the horizon and the isle of cats was no more than a bad dream.

* * *

It had been a week to forget.

To help things along, Teizo suggested a Tuesday night rendezvous. Not without her reservations, she stepped off Nankin-machi Street and made her way to the end of the alley, to where the *Bar Bon Voyage* sign sizzled like a beacon to all of Chinatown's lost and needy. Beneath its orange neon glow, she hesitated. Her midnight blue one-piece dress no longer pinched. She took a deep breath and pushed on the door.

A chorus of greetings from the bar staff rang out as she made her way across the low-lit air-conditioned room. He was seated at the end of the counter—early as always—a glass of chilled sake, this time set in a *masu* wooden box, before him.

'I wasn't sure you'd come,' he said.

'Neither was I.' She slid on to the stool and to the bartender said, 'Soda with lemon, please'.

He showed no surprise. Instead, he asked, 'How did it go?'

'As expected, they fired me.'

Her drink order arrived. 'When life deals you a lemon, make lemonade.' She raised her glass to his, he reciprocated, and they drank quietly.

'Management called it *dereliction of duty*,' she said.

'How did they find out?'

'A nice young woman in accounts accidentally told her colleague, who told her colleague ... who told Goto, who called my mother. She had no idea she was meant to be at a funeral of a brother she never had.'

Teizo listened, nodding thoughtfully. Two days earlier, aboard the ferry, she'd called and told him everything. The outpouring had brought relief. Then, following her meeting with the hotel's human resources manager that morning, reality had hit her like a punch on the jaw. She now stood on the edge of an abyss, staring down.

'So, why not go solo?' he said.

'Pardon me?'

'Start your own business.'

'A hotel?'

He was watching her now, a smile forming on his lips. Her eyes widened. She shook her head and laughed out loud. 'Oh no … no can do.'

'Why not? Full-time, flexible hours, charge what you want. This city's full of troubled people.'

'Do I look like someone ready to start my own private investigation company?'

'You once asked me—do I look like a private detective? Well, my answer still stands.'

'I haven't been exactly triumphant.'

'You haven't failed either.'

'Some would call that luck.'

'You're not superstitious. And besides, your clients pay you for your efforts—not results.'

She sipped her lemon-soda.

He lifted his glass from the *masu*, tipped the overflow from the box into his glass and drank. A moment of contemplative calm hung in the air between them.

'I'm curious,' he said, at last. 'What happened to the young woman from Ikuta Shrine.'

'Sora Koba? The priest found out she'd been working two part-time jobs. The other was at a yaki-tori joint in Osaka—her boss got her pregnant.'

Teizo's eyebrows arched.

'And it doesn't end there,' she said.

'No?'

'The priest confided in me. Tomoya Nakata has since asked her to marry him, regardless.'

'What did she say?'

'Yes.'

Teizo shook his head. 'This has Goddess Wakahirume no mikoto's fingerprints all over it.'

'When Koba told him she was pregnant by another man, he was heartbroken … perhaps that's why he ran away to Manabeshima, to do some soul-searching. God knows how he managed that on an island overrun by cats.'

'She must really love him.'

In the bar mirror reflection, her gaze found his. 'Teizo—you couldn't script this stuff.'

* * *

She awoke before dawn and made breakfast for her mother and daughter.

A wall of worry had denied her sleep. She felt tired and drawn out. She had four weeks to find new employment, a job that would pay enough to support her mother, daughter, and all the bills in between. Her thoughts turned to Reiko Ogino, Danno, and the paranoid president of Tokai Pearls Limited, and for one crazy moment, she wondered if there might be a position at one of their pearl-sorting desks.

By 8.30 a.m. she was on duty behind the Orient Hotel's long cedar desk when Tsuro, the night manager, handed her a bundle of envelopes. 'Fan mail,' he smiled. 'Enjoy your day.'

There were more in her mailbox. They contained letters of thanks, encouragement and condolence, but most surprisingly, inquiry. Their senders wanted to know about her services, rates, and her availability to meet to discuss matters of a 'sensitive nature'. They were signed by staff from hotel catering, housekeeping, maintenance, and accounts sections—people she had never met before. There was even a letter from one of the hotel directors, apologizing for her dismissal, but keenly interested in her services for a 'private matter' that had been bothering him for quite some time.

Over the coming days, more letters arrived. These Goto passed on with disdain.

The following Tuesday evening, as she made her way along the esplanade towards the train station, she sighted Teizo. He stood among the other old fishers casting from the edge of the wharf. He wore his usual sun-bleached uniform of jeans and a T-shirt, with a white towel wrapped around his suntanned neck.

She had to admit, even from a distance, he was a good-looking man. She wanted to tell him so, but she held her tongue, reasoning that it would only embarrass him in front of his fellow fishers.

Creeping up behind him, she whispered in his ear: 'How's the fishing business?'

'How's the job-hunting business?' he said without turning.

'Like you, I'm still angling.'

She stood beside him now, taking in the shipyards and submarine docks of Kawasaki Heavy Industries, the Mosaic Shopping Mall and its slow-turning Ferris wheel, and finally the Port Tower where tour boats came and went from the ferry terminal.

'I've been thinking about what you said the other night,' she said.

'And?'

'You're right. This city *is* filled with troubled people.'

'Sounds to me like trouble could be a full-time business.'

'How does Mami Suzuki, Pearl City Private Eye Inc. sound?'

'Perfect.' He reeled in his line, folded his rod, and shouldered his icebox. 'How do we celebrate?'

'With lemon-sodas. Then, we'll take it from there....'

Acknowledgements

My sincere thanks to Goro Koyama of Japan PI Inc. and Makoto Ohara of Ohara Research Security for enlightening me on the ways of big city private investigators; to Deborah Iwabuchi, Yoshiko Nakamura, Taro Starbuck, Shigeaki 'Kit' Kitaoka, Takako Kiyose, Rhonda Payne, Ruth Barber, Denise Fenwick, Richard Harrison, Kevin Ballou, Ashley Rowe, Catherine Rowe, and Claudia Rowe, for their feedback and encouragement; to the talented Levente Szabó for his striking cover art and rendering of Mami Suzuki the way I envisioned her; to Nora Nazerene Abu Bakar, Ishani Bhattacharya, Garima Bhatt, Chaitanya Srivastava, Rupal Vyas, Swadha Singh, Divya Gaur, Pallavi Narayan, Arpita Dasgupta, Rachna Pratap, and the publishing team at Penguin Random House SEA for their support; and to my editor, Amberdawn Manaois, whose keen eye and sense of story have helped me to sharpen my own. Finally, a sumo-sized *arigatou-gozaimasu!* to Edgar Award-winning mystery writer, Naomi Hirahara, for taking time out of her busy schedule to read this story and offer her thoughts.